D0378358

Terminal Grill

Terminal Grill

Rosemary Aubert

The publication of *Terminal Grill* has been generously supported by the Canada Council for the Arts and the Ontario Arts Council.

Canada Council for the Arts | Conseil des Arts du Canada

Author's photograph: Doug Purdon
Cover design: Sarah Beaudin
Editor: John Calabro
Typography: Grey Wolf Typography

Library and Archives Canada Cataloguing in Publication

Aubert, Rosemary
Terminal grill / Rosemary Aubert.

Issued also in electronic format.
ISBN 978-1-927443-43-9

I. Title.

PS8551.U24T47 2013 C813'.54 C2013-900388-6

Published by Quattro Books Inc.
382 College Street
Toronto, Ontario, M5T 1S8
www.quattrobooks.ca

Printed in Canada

This book is dedicated to my dear friend,
Sandra Rabinovitch.

1987

CHAPTER ONE

To MATTHEW, ALL THE days of the week are the same, and on each, no matter how busy he seems, he has only two things to do: to keep himself from thinking about what he has become and to find a place to sleep for the night.

I met him at a wake.

Not a real wake. A poetry reading on a warm spring Sunday in a seedy bar in what used to be the garment district. And I can't say I really met him—only that I noticed him. For, like a lot of the other shady characters that slink into and out of the shadows and the limelight of the poetry world, he seemed familiar to me.

The wake was for a weathered, wizened, beat-up old poet I used to see wandering the streets in summer with his typewriter tucked under his arm. The hundred or so who stuffed themselves into the dusty old bar to honour him gone were the same ones who'd drunk and argued and fought with him on a thousand afternoons like this one in a dozen other watering holes as cozy and greasy and sad.

Every chair in the place was taken. I was sitting with friends—all men—and when one of them got up to go to the bar, this oddly-familiar stranger, who had been standing a few yards away, stepped up and asked me if he could sit down.

We were by the front windows of the place, windows heavily curtained by dark, torn drapes. Every once in a while, someone would open one of the doors that led to the street, admitting a chiaroscuro shot of spring sun.

I'd had only one beer, but my head was light from not eating all day and from the affectionate attention of my male poet friends who teased and flattered me. No one said anything to the stranger. He smiled pleasantly toward us all and turned his attention to the band.

It was a pretty amateurish group and before long, they started to sound as though it were playing the same song over and over. A lot of poets had already read, but my friends were still waiting their turn and a lot more were going to read before they got it, judging from the program.

I grew impatient. People came and went—not all of them friendly—most of them pressing up against those of us who sat at the table, getting in the way of the stranger who had to look around them to catch even a glimpse of the band.

But though he got up to get a beer now and then, nobody asked me whether his seat was taken, and each time he returned, he sat still, not at all bothered by the comings and goings of others, and listening with what seemed some care. Once or twice, he complimented members of the band as they stepped off the stage—which in these fairly primitive surroundings really just meant stepping away from the mic. And they responded to him, which I thought interesting, since musicians tend not to take compliments seriously at all unless the compliments come from other musicians. I tried hard to remember where I might have seen him before, but I had no luck.

Then the poets came back on stage. One after another they read their works. I started to find it hard to listen to them. Finally, though, the last of my friends got up to read, leaving me with the stranger at the table. I began to grow more conscious of his presence, as though we were suddenly together. Out of the blue, he mentioned that he was from out of town.

"Oh, yeah?" I said, "From where?"

"Hartford, Connecticut," he answered.

"Insurance capital of the world," I threw out, and he nodded. "A couple of great American artists were into insurance," I added, "Wallace Stevens, Charles Ives. Ives wrote the best-selling textbook ever written on the insurance business …"

His face took on a look of uncertainty, and I thought he was probably thinking, *What a little know-it-all this one is!* It occurred to me to wonder whether I'd mixed up New Haven and Hartford, never having been to either.

But the man opposite me said very seriously, "I think the days of using Ives are past. The techniques are all different now." Again he smiled, a smile that was boyish and easy. "But before—well, there's a story I just love. It's about a little kid whose father has died. One day the insurance man comes to the door and the little kid just happens to be the one who answers. His mom is in the kitchen and he runs to her and says, 'Mom, we just got a letter from Daddy'. 'A letter from Daddy?' the mother says, upset, 'But honey, I told you—' But then the little boy holds up a nice fat cheque from the insurance company—"

"Shit!" I said, and we both laughed.

Though I had no more beer, I started to feel good. I started to feel that life was treating me just fine. Here in this room were plenty of men who obviously found me worthy of their attention—including this dark and good-looking stranger. Up on stage now was one of my friends and waiting for him to finish was another and both of them were good poets and interesting companions. I was ready to accept that all my exes and friends and might-have-beens were the only men in my life. I was okay. I was ready to call it a day, ready to take this warm glow back to my cold basement apartment. Ready to quit while I was ahead.

But it seemed wrong to leave in the middle of a poetry set. Then it seemed wrong to walk out on the band. So the afternoon wore on. My friends came back to the table. Someone came over and invited them to join "everyone" for Chinese food across the street as soon as the wake was over. She nodded toward me, too.

But all I wanted was to get something to eat fast and to go home by myself, satisfied with the afternoon and determined to spend the evening studying for an exam in my night-school criminology course.

Every time somebody cracked the darkness with a splice of sun from the door, I edged closer to standing up and getting out.

Only, I couldn't get out without crawling over the good-looking stranger, plus a couple of my friends, all of whom were now on the same side of the table between me and the path to the door.

At long last, the afternoon's program ended with a tape—a long, gravelly posthumous speech from the day's dead poet. It was a voice from the grave. From the streets. From drunk alleys and garbage can meals and filthy doorways and fleabag rooms. A voice so familiar to everybody in the room—everybody who'd been yelled at, cajoled, convinced, stunned by the old guy—that all of a sudden the wake was for real.

The roomful of poets emptied fast, but with an impressive lot of silence.

Into the spaces left slipped the usual habitués of the place. I sensed my friends talking to each other, but I wasn't paying close attention, because the stranger had asked me whether I was a poet—a question it took me a minute to think about. They got up and started to walk away. One of them turned back and said, "We'll be back to get you to go over for supper."

There was now only me and the stranger in that whole section of the pub. "Is that your man?" he asked me.

And knowing full well exactly how it would sound, nevertheless I said, "I have no man."

At first I thought my friend had meant it when he said they were coming back. But more and more poets left, more and more neighbourhood types—seasoned drinkers in green workpants and checkered shirts—filled spaces at the rickety tables, though no one came into the corner where we sat.

A waitress came and cleared our table of all but the two beers that sat in front of my new friend. He helped her, gathering glasses and bottles and empty packages from cigarettes. He smiled at her, and she smiled back.

"So," he said, in a voice I now noticed was smooth and very deep and slightly accented with the unmistakable tones of New England, "are you a poet?"

I looked down, the question always embarrassing me. "Yeah," I said, "but I didn't read today."

"I didn't think you were a poet," he said. "They all seemed so anxious to get up there and stay there as long as they could—hogging the spotlight. You don't seem like that."

I, of course, could say nothing to that.

"Anyway," he went on. "I'm glad I didn't miss you. I got here late. I heard about the wake, and I knew I better come."

He spoke about it as if it were as much a wake as one held in a funeral home. The poet in question had been buried a few months now, so …

"You knew him, then?" I asked.

"Knew him? Oh yes, yes, sure."

Across the room, a well-built, slender man with wild blond hair dyed lighter in front stood up and got ready to leave the pub. "Know him, too," the stranger said.

"I do, too," I smiled. The man was a poet and rock singer whom I'd known when the wild hair had been curls and the hard rock songs had been lonely folk ballads. He was on his way to fame now.

"Bet he doesn't talk to us," my companion said, and I noticed bitterness in his voice. It was a little surprising because he seemed such an even-tempered, almost gentle man, as far as one could tell from a couple of hours' nearly silent acquaintance.

"I don't think he can see us here in the corner," I commented as both of us watched the man leave without so much as a glance our way.

"Are you a musician yourself?" I asked, curiosity finally getting the best of me.

The man turned and looked me full in the face. He had a strange expression, one compounded of shyness and something else. "Yes," he said, "as a matter of fact I'm a pianist with Neil Young."

I looked away from him. I was ignorant of any specific knowledge of that kind of music, but something struck me funny about a famous musician having a pianist. "Yes," the man said, "that's why I'm here. Neil's doing a video. We've been at it almost two weeks and now we've got eight days left."

"I guess you've been with him a while?" I asked, not really knowing what to say.

"Seven years," he said. And he launched into a long, complicated genealogy of bands the way a historian will sometimes launch into an explanation of the bloodline of foreign kings. I recognized some of the names, and the way he talked was the way I remembered people talking about bands when I did know about such things, but for the most part, I didn't know what the hell he was talking about.

But I'd have to have been really stupid not to have known that Neil Young was famous and that anybody who travelled with him, as this man was claiming he did, had to be pretty near famous himself.

"Neil lives in L.A. now," he offered.

"So that's why you live in the States?" I asked, a little nervous now, but not wanting to end our conversation.

"Yes. So I'm just up here for a little while longer."

Part of me was thinking how lucky it was to have met somebody as charming and handsome and important as this.

CHAPTER TWO

THE BEAUTIFUL, LIKE THE rich, are different.

I couldn't help noticing as we spoke just how beautiful Matthew was—a white lion with a black mane. Pale, slight, but with a high-cheekboned face that seemed sometimes boyish, sometimes harshly masculine. His eyes had a startling, dark intensity that set off the wild long tumble of his black curls. He wore an impressive sweater on the front of which was embroidered a panther in dozens of subtle shades of thread, including a shot of shining gold.

When it became evident that my friends were not going to return, Matthew sort of offered in a hinting way to help me find them and I sort of hinted that I'd rather go somewhere with him. It worked. He told me he knew a little place not far away and was more or less headed that way now and that I would be welcome to come along. Again, I felt flattered. He seemed very much younger than me and very suave and very good-looking and very well-dressed in the navy raincoat he donned as we left the bar.

Out in the afternoon sun, still brilliant now at half-past six, I saw, to my surprise, that he was quite nervous. He looked at me with a sort of sidelong glance and laughed and said he liked the way the colour of my hair looked in the sun. I asked him if we should take the bus, assuming that we would, but he said he would rather take a cab and that he always took cabs when he'd been drinking a few. I thought this an odd comment from a man from out of town and wondered whether he was implying that he had a car.

We walked up Spadina just a few metres and saw an empty cab parked in front of Mr. Submarine. Matthew said that obviously the driver had gone in for a coffee and that he'd be out any minute. There was such authority in his voice that even so simple a comment seemed an impressive display.

But we waited for a bit, and the driver didn't come out, so Matthew hailed another cab. We got in, and as we sped up Spadina I felt young and free and a little wild to have gone off with a man as young and handsome and—maybe—as important as this. By the time we got to Bloor and Madison, a few minutes' drive away, I was already willing to ignore the fact that I was almost sure that Matthew had inadvertently referred to himself in the third person, as if he were not Matthew at all, or as if he had momentarily forgotten that Matthew was who he was supposed to be.

The bar he'd chosen was a very nice one I'd seen from the outside many times and had often wanted to go into, though not alone. So I'd never been. It was new, but decorated in a fairly traditional English-pub style. It was close enough to the University of Toronto to be a student/graduate bar, and it was crowded. Nonetheless, Matthew strode in with confidence and immediately found us an acceptable table. I found it reassuring that the waiters and some others in the bar seemed to nod to Matthew as if they knew him. I did not ask myself why I needed to be reassured.

We sat in the bar and talked for a very long time. I asked Matthew a few questions about his career, and again he said he was part of a back-up band that travelled everywhere with Neil Young and that they'd been in town for a total of three weeks minus the eight days they had left and that they were working on a video. He mentioned the studio—the address sounded vaguely familiar. He mentioned that a well-known children's show was finishing up taping when they had arrived to begin their shoot. I asked him if they were striking the set when his people had arrived. When I used the word "striking"—

not one the uninitiated might be expected to use— Matthew registered pleased surprise.

In the cab we had talked about the only mutual acquaintances we shared in Toronto. One was the musician who had failed to say hello to us at the wake, whose name was Dill. The other was a woman named Barbara who'd once been that musician's lover. Barbara was an eccentric and outspoken woman, a poet herself. The only other person both Matthew and I had known was the dead poet. Now as we talked, I asked him where he was staying, expecting him to name a hotel.

Instead, he spun a long tale about a magazine writer, whose name was, again, vaguely familiar, saying that the writer had asked his advice when writing a review about the work of Dill and Barbara, a review that Matthew implied was very critical of Dill, since Matthew didn't like Dill's work. He said that the writer, who, according to him, worked for a well-known Toronto magazine, was out of town and that he was staying at the home of her and her husband because it was nicer than staying at a hotel. He then smiled and added a touching little detail: he said they had a bird that he was looking after for them, a cockatiel. I didn't ask him where this apartment was, but he volunteered the information that it was near Maple Leaf Gardens.

As we spoke, Matthew kept saying he preferred not to talk about his career or his music. But he did talk a lot about many things. I was very hungry and ordered a sandwich, which I ate, and a basket of French fries, which I was too excited to eat, even though I still felt starved. Matthew ordered nothing but beer and wouldn't touch the food I'd ordered and offered to him.

On and on we talked. Mostly, I listened. When I mentioned my interest in criminology, he told me that he used to do benefit concerts in prisons. He said that one time, the band got the time of a concert wrong and ended up at a prison one hour late only to discover that the warden had made the men put up chairs for the concert, sit in them for nearly an hour, then take them all down again—then refused under any circumstances to let the concert go on when the band arrived. He said the band was so furious about this that they tore up the town.

I was tremendously impressed not only with this story, but with the apparent sensitivity of the teller.

He told me that he no longer did benefit concerts, though, he said, he'd done Farm Aid. He said that now—and this was a recurring theme throughout our days—he was planning to go to South Africa "to educate." He mentioned a prominent Canadian journalist and said the man had promised to keep an eye on him and to write about him if he should be killed.

I knew so little about the kind of music he claimed to be working on that to question him would have been rude. So I kept my peace, except to say I felt there were causes closer to home he could take up instead. He said nothing to that. But he did quite clearly say about going to Africa, "Matthew says it's dangerous."

His slips into oddness, the flamboyance of his claims, and the darting intensity of his black eyes seemed to be warning me. But I have spent enough hours among poets, musicians and the marginally insane to believe it's safe to give them the benefit of the doubt. To wait for riches ...

He was so confident, so intelligent and so charming that I was willing to risk his being strange. He talked a great deal about his family. He told me his oldest brother had been a hockey player. As with the story of Matthew's connection with the band he said he played with, he offered me a genealogy of hockey, eventually leading to the Hartford Whalers—

of whom I knew just as much as I knew about Neil Young. He said that his brother had retired seven years before and that Matthew had bought his house in Hartford and had lived there since. He had been raised in Toronto, he said.

I noticed as he spoke that his knowledge of Toronto and his accent seemed exactly right for the facts he was relating.

He spoke of this brother, the eldest of the four sons that made up his family, as if they had been quite close. The brother now lived in L.A. with his wife, a woman of whom Matthew clearly was not enamoured. He spoke of having visited this oldest brother often, implying in a vague way that though he hadn't seen him in a couple years, he still kept in touch with him and was closer to him than to anyone else in the family. The brother, he said, was called Daniel.

Of the next brother, Paul, he said practically nothing. Of the next, Sam, the third oldest, he said that he'd been in bad trouble with the FBI, that at one point a rich man who was his friend had bailed him out of one scrape by confronting the FBI and pretty much chasing them away from his Toronto home, where Sam was holed up. "Then," Matthew said, "Sam met a woman—"

He leaned close to me and said, "I've never told this to anybody before, but I can talk to you. The fact is, I liked Sam's wife. I liked her so much that I felt I was in love with her myself. Not that we did anything—it was just that, well, she changed Sam's life. She changed his life completely …"

Two things struck me about this passionate revelation. The first was how desperately impressed Matthew seemed to be at the phenomenon of having one's life "changed completely." The other was how intensely he seemed to identify with Sam. I thought again about his referring to himself in the third person. A strange, unwelcome thought flitted in and out of my mind. The thought that maybe I should allow myself to wonder which brother my companion really was.

CHAPTER THREE

"I WAS THE YOUNGEST but there would have been another. When I was four my mother had a miscarriage in the driveway of our house. Sam and I saw it, but my father would never tell us what happened. After that my mother overdosed on pills and tried to kill herself. I've hated pills ever since."

He spoke of his father's gruff domination of the family, of his mother's passivity, which greatly disturbed him. He mentioned his father's business and his special love for his grandmother, who had provided for his early musical education.

He told me about his unusual hobby. He said he was an angler—a fly-fisher. He mentioned Izaak Walton and I piped up, "author of *The Compleat Angler*." His face lit up and he said my knowing that "blew his socks off."

He talked and talked and I listened, enraptured. "Do you mind if I tell you something?" he said in a suddenly personal tone, and fascinated, I leaned closer.

"Of course not. What?"

He smiled as he said softly, "I didn't like the way your friends deserted you like that."

There was something odd about the comment. I didn't understand why he should think I would mind. Except that he seemed a very polite man at all times. I thought it was very nice of him to care enough to mention such a thing. I apologized for my friends and Matthew went on talking.

A couple of times he excused himself and disappeared off somewhere behind me, presumably to go to the washroom. So did I. And each time, I asked myself what I was doing with such a young, attractive, successful, exciting man. I wondered where this was going to lead. And then I wondered whether I cared.

He told me he was thirty-five but that most people took him to be younger. He started to explain something about his age that made it sound as though he thought I was younger than him. I stopped him with a laugh and told him, "I'm older than you. I'm forty, though with me, too, most people don't realize it."

He laughed. We joked about Dorian Gray.

For a while a blues band played and we listened. He said he recognized one of the players as a famous old-timer. I had no way of knowing anything about the man, myself, but Matthew sounded like he knew all about him.

Hours passed. Our waitress left, Matthew paying her first for my food and our beers and his cigarettes. He wouldn't hear of my paying for anything and he seemed to have plenty of cash. Another waiter took over our table. Matthew leaned across and said to me, "You're very nice—" and of course I said, "So are you …."

The blues band long departed, Matthew suggested we move toward the piano in the part of the room where they'd been. He wanted to play for me, as had been his intention in bringing me to that bar. Matthew signaled the waiter and told him we were moving. I wasn't sure why he did this, but it seemed like a nice touch. He was obviously a man of some polish.

We moved nearer to the piano and sat on high stools at a round table. Now, instead of being across from each other, we were side by side. I noticed that Matthew moved gradually closer and that once in a while, his thigh brushed mine. I didn't pull away.

His singing voice was wonderful—surprisingly gruff and full of some elusive emotion that teetered between pain and youthful innocence. The minute he touched the piano, he seemed lost in the music, though he had a professional's habit of looking away from the keyboard toward whatever audience might be listening. I was listening. And watching. He looked different when he played, not as handsome and somehow smaller. But he seemed more at ease with himself, too.

He sang three old traditional blues numbers, a couple of which were familiar to me. One had a line that went, "Throw your big leg over me, mama—don't know when I'm gonna feel this good again."

I loved the sound of him. But he was rusty. Not at all like a man who'd spent the past two weeks playing in a video every day.

The people in the bar didn't seem to mind, though. They clapped and shouted out for him to play more, and when he sat down beside me again, a couple of people stopped by to tell him how much they'd enjoyed what he'd done.

He ordered more beers for us and we talked on. He told me his parents hadn't responded to him as a child and he told me, too, how he'd once taken a helicopter trip over the Grand Canyon and been so bowled over by what he saw that he'd asked his girlfriend of the time to go with him and do it again, but that she wasn't very impressed. He said that if he could have had children, he would always have been careful to respond to every single thing they showed him with enthusiasm so that their excitement about life would never be dampened. When he spoke about children, his whole body seemed to come alive and his voice was full of feeling.

I couldn't help but be enormously touched by this. It brought out the maternal instinct in me—toward him. I asked him why he spoke of having children as something beyond him, seeing as he was still so young.

"I can't have children for various reasons," he said with a slightly evasive smile, and I feared I'd been impolite, though he showed no irritation at my question at all.

We'd been together since four and it was nearly eleven. Matthew insisted I have another beer, though it seemed to me I'd been drinking for a very long time, not that I felt drunk in the least. But noticing the time, I realized I should take out my contact lenses before they became permanently melded to my eyeballs. I made a joke about it and excused myself to go to the washroom yet again. Matthew said of course, but that before I went, he wanted a favour.

"What?" I asked, more touched than nervous.

"I want you to kiss me," he said. "Would you do that?"

The request seemed touching and charming and inviting. It also seemed slick. But I let his lips briefly touch mine.

When I returned I told him I couldn't see very much but that vanity prevented my putting my glasses on. He told me to put them on by all means, and that he would like me with them on just as much as he liked me without them. He asked for another kiss and got it.

Then he started a new conversation. He said he couldn't understand how a nice man like him and a nice woman like me could be alone the way we were. He said he couldn't believe I didn't have a husband. There was about these comments the same slickness as there'd been with the first kiss. I could have told him lots of reasons why people like us could be alone, allowing our thighs to press against the thighs of strangers. We could be crazy. We could be sick. We could be liars. I could easily have had a husband and he could easily have had a wife. Maybe more than one. Or each of us could also have had someone at home with a body more or less exactly like our own.

But I said nothing. And when he said, "After three weeks all my faults become obvious …," as if that explained why he was alone, I thought to myself, "After three weeks you'll be in Hartford or Africa and I'll have forgotten this conversation."

He wanted to talk about the happiness of simple people—married people. He told me about the couples he sometimes saw in the lounges he played in. It sounded as though he'd toured the whole country playing in piano bars. He told me how happy and satisfied with each other some of the middle-aged and older couples were, how the women in small towns would dress up just to go out with their husbands to some local place. He told me that everywhere he went, he liked to go down into the audience during his breaks and sit with some older couple and chat with them.

He told me how one charming old couple had chided him about how thin he was. He said they left and he went on to play his last set, but that during the set, the old man had come back and put a bag on the stage, then disappeared. When the set was over and Matthew opened the bag, he discovered two fat cheeseburgers.

He talked like a man who'd played five thousand one-night stands in five thousand one-horse towns.

We talked and drank some more. "I've only written one hit song in my life," he said. He got up and went back to the piano and did a few bars of vocal and instrumental introduction that I'd never heard before, then segued into the main body of a song that I recognized as one of my very favourites, a song my brother had played for me countless times. I was dumbfounded.

That Matthew should have written this song among all the possible songs in the world seemed the most wonderful stroke of fate. The old familiar words that had rung in my ears in my brother's soft sweet voice now tumbled there in the rough voice of the stranger, and I was spellbound, wishing the moment could go on forever.

But he finished and moved back to the table. Up till then, I had only touched him accidentally. Now I reached out and caressed his arm and told him that the song had been special to me for a very long time.

He was very pleased with my reaction and we talked about the history of the song, how he had felt, when, at the age of nineteen, he'd had it recorded by a major folk singer of the sixties.

In the middle of this conversation, he left once again, and when he was gone, I thought about things a bit. When he came back, I told him a story. It had to do with a friend of mine, a woman who'd been a folksinger in the sixties, too. It had to do with a ring she had at the centre of which was a magnificent pearl of great size. The pearl was beautiful beyond description, but my friend always claimed to hate that ring—because nobody would believe the pearl was real.

Matthew smiled at me and said, "That's a very nice story."

Somehow he worked the conversation about to the subject of coffee, and he wondered whether we could go somewhere and make some. I thought he was inviting me to go back with him, and a thousand nos and yeses battled in my head.

Then I realized he sounded as though he were inviting himself back to my place, though I couldn't be exactly sure.

He stood and helped me with my coat, then put his stylish raincoat on over the panther sweater.

Beside the golden eyes of the cat was a string of what looked like Chinese letters painstakingly embroidered in red. He saw me looking at the sweater and said, "This sweater was made especially for me by the Japanese designer Yashimoto. There's only one like it in the whole world ...."

I felt my eyes widen, but I said nothing. Matthew gestured toward the line of red letters. His eyes were deep and soft in the dim light of the bar. "The letters are a sort of poem," he said.

"What does the poem say?" I asked.

Matthew smiled. "It says, 'The night is a panther ...'"

CHAPTER FOUR

Out in the street I asked him if he was in fact inviting himself back to my place. He hedged a bit but didn't deny it. I said it would be okay but that I lived in a basement apartment and that other people lived in the house and would be there, too. That was all right with him.

We walked the short distance to Bloor, hailed a cab going in the wrong direction, got inside and made ourselves comfortable as the driver pulled a good Uie in the middle of the street that was still busy at eleven p.m.

The cab, like no other I'd seen in Toronto, but like those I'd seen in Detroit, had a bullet-proof shield completely separating the driver from his passengers. Matthew was appalled at this and said the very sight of the thing inspired an ugly paranoia. We talked about that shield most of the fifteen or twenty minutes it took to get to my place. When we did get to my house, Matthew wondered how he was supposed to pay. He didn't wonder long. A little door, like a chute, popped open at a level with our eyes and Matthew slid through a twenty. He seemed to have no end of twenties, though he was careful to tell the driver that it was a large bill and he also refused, on principle because of the shield, to leave a tip.

I led him down the side of my house past the basement windows toward the back door. The house was completely dark, but I wasn't nervous. As I let him in, I warned him to watch his head, as the headroom of the door was too low for all those over five-foot-five.

He came in and immediately hung up his coat. I have never known a man more careful with his clothes—as if he were conscious at all times that any mistreatment—the slightest wrinkle, the smallest tear, the tiniest spot—could have major consequences.

He turned away from the coat rack at the bottom of the stairs and at once his eye fell on an eight-by-ten baby portrait of me. "Who's that baby?" he wanted to know, and I sensed strong emotion behind his question, perhaps a note of fear, as if he thought this baby might be mine and that there might be a husband lurking somewhere despite my previous protestations to the contrary.

"It's me," I said with a little laugh, moving closer to him.

And suddenly, I was in his arms, the whole length of me drawn close up against him, either by my will or his or both. His body fit perfectly against mine, and it felt totally natural to hold him, to feel the slender yet substantial muscles of his shoulders in the clasp of my arms.

But I pulled away and went to make the coffee. It was going to be instant, which was all I had. But he said that was okay. It was a remarkable thing about Matthew that, much as he spoke in the most intimate detail of the finer things in life, he was always gracious in accepting anything one offered him—except food.

I had told him that, as well as taking night courses and working part-time, I was an author, and I led him to a portion of the basement between the large furnished room and kitchenette that formed most of it and the washroom. In this unfinished in-between space were some shelves and a workbench on which I kept a row of copies of my books. He stood beside me and listened with the politeness of an obedient child as I showed him the various editions. He didn't seem genuinely interested, but he showed no impatience.

Since we'd met at a poetry event, I reached up and took down for him a copy of my poetry collection.

This little space was lit by a single, bare, overhead bulb, and by its light, Matthew was suddenly studying my face. "I didn't notice you have such beautiful eyes," he said, his own eyes blazing.

There was such intensity in his expression that it struck me uncomfortably as the expression of a good actor who could be just a smidgen better. It occurred to me to wonder how this man could have been talking to me for the past five hours and not notice my eyes. Other men had noticed them in a lot shorter time than that. I grinned a little condescendingly.

Matthew reached out and touched me, his hands at my waist, then sliding up beneath my sweater.

I was tempted to let him remove it, which was what he quite clearly had in mind. Instead, I pulled away and told him I'd better check the coffee.

I poured it for us. I had no milk. He said that was just fine. We sat on my futon, which I kept folded like a couch, and I told him I had a problem—which was that I considered it against my principles to have sex with someone I'd just met. There was no question of presumption in my comment. The appropriateness of it was perfectly obvious to us both.

Matthew's expression was soft, handsome, boyish and—it seemed to me—a trifle desperate. "Let me spend the night here and just be with you," he said with a sidelong glance. "I can do that, you know—"

There was no way I was going to say no. It seemed to me a long time since I had had the warmth of a man beside me in bed.

Within minutes we were undressed and the futon was pulled out double-size and we were sitting beneath the covers talking.

When we talked, his striking intelligence was obvious. When we touched, he was so tender, so accommodating. Nothing seemed to annoy him, insult him, anger him. He asked me nothing about myself, and, since I wanted to talk about my life as little as possible, not wanting to mar the day and the night with reality, I offered nothing.

His body was very lean and of absolutely perfect proportion. He was Michelangelo's David, as if the cold artful stone had magically become warm, familiar, pliant flesh. Easily the most beautiful body I'd ever seen.

When I removed my clothes, he seemed dumbstruck, though I laughed at his sudden insistence that I, too, was beautiful. He seemed never to tire of trying to convince me that I was a beauty. "I didn't know," he kept saying, "I couldn't tell by the way you dress. I only looked at your face. You are such a beauty. Such a beauty."

For a while he lay with his back to me, smoking a cigarette over the crafted clay bowl I'd given him to use as an ashtray, which sat on the rug at the side of the futon beside the small table that held a lamp and the baby portrait of me. I lay alongside him, propped on my elbow, as he was, and with my chin on his shoulder. It felt as though we'd known each other all our lives, so casually did we lie together.

Over his shoulder, he said, "Why don't you dress like a beauty?"

"I don't know how beauties dress."

I knew he would not try to make me change my mind about making love with him, and he didn't. But somehow we spent a great deal of time touching. And before we slept, he whispered, "Will you promise me something?"

"Yeah. Sure. What?"

"Will you let me come back tomorrow night and make love to you then?"

I smiled into the happy darkness. "Okay," I said. "Okay."

CHAPTER FIVE

In the morning I had to throw him out at 7:30.

I had a business appointment at 8:30 and I wanted a little time to myself. Though we had gone to sleep quite late, he made no complaint about getting up so early. He dressed—he'd placed his clothes neatly on a chair. He asked me if I still wanted to see him that evening. I said yes but that I had to go to school and wouldn't be free until sometime between 8:30 and 9:30. He said he still wanted to see me, too, and that the time was no problem for him.

I told him a little about my course and that I was nervous about going to class because I knew the teacher was planning to hand back essays we'd done.

When he left, I missed him. I went to my appointment and then to my afternoon job, but before I went into my office, which was in a large shopping mall, I stopped at a well-stocked record store and checked every single Neil Young record—lots of them. I discovered that Neil Young did indeed have a pianist credited on some of his records. But that pianist was not Matthew.

Unreasoning panic filled me. I remembered all the odd little things about him, including the two times he'd referred to himself in the third person. All I could think of was that he might have wandered into the poetry event at which I'd met him straight from the Clarke—a mental hospital about a ten-minute walk from the bar in which I'd first talked to him.

But I had no time even to think about that. I got to my office and did a full afternoon without even getting up to call Ruth, my best friend, to tell her what was going on.

Between work and getting on the subway for school, I had only a five-minute break. I ran to the nearest phone away from the office, which was in a commuter bus terminal in the basement of the neighbouring plaza. I could hardly hear myself, let alone Ruth as I tried to tell her about Matthew, the sounds of bus after bus being announced blaring across the echoing expanse of the terminal.

I told her as fast as I could where I'd met Matthew and what he'd told me about himself. She listened patiently to my breathy, shouted story, then promised to see if she could find out anything about him from a friend of hers who'd spent some time in the rock music business several years before.

When I told her my doubts, she said there might be plenty of explanations for the fact that Matthew's name wasn't on the albums. She said he sounded like an interesting guy. She told me to keep calm, to have a good time, and to use safes.

So on the way to school, at the expense of possibly being late, I stopped at a drugstore and bought some.

It was nearly impossible to pay attention to the lecturer at class, even though the teacher was a noted guest from the States. No matter what he said, all I could think of was how much longer it would be until I would see Matthew again.

Finally, I snuck out the back door, ran to the subway station, hopped on the train and tore across town toward the Terminal Grill.

The Terminal Grill was a perfect neighbourhood bar five minutes from my house. It was probably built between the wars and had never been renovated. I'd heard an old customer swear that there used to be a huge ceiling fan, but the waitress argued so strongly that nothing has ever been changed at the Terminal, that the old customer backed down, saying, "I could have sworn, but I guess I must be wrong."

It looked like a diner, only longer and wider with lots of windows, a bar with stools, and booths with green marble tables and patched red banquette seats. The menus were covered with padded dark red plastic that in the old days used to be called leatherette, and the faded scraps of gold that clung to some of them must once have been the emblazoned name of the place.

There was a jukebox at every table. Once a year or so, a man came and changed the songs.

It was adjacent to a subway station and across the street from one of the TTC barns. During all the hours that it was open—probably from seven a.m. to midnight, the shift of the owner and the waitress and the cook—uniformed TTC drivers came in and out for take-out or to sit for a meal. Alone, they always seemed to be reading. But together they were a boisterous lot.

The other habitués were an assortment of neighbourhood drunks who shouted insults to each other across the aisle between the booths and the bar or the double row of six booths in the back. Or who discussed politics so energetically that it made a person feel good to live in a democracy, just so everybody had a right to his say.

On Friday nights, there were also the genteel poor—old couples come for a night out, a feast of five-dollar pork chops complete with soup, crackers, roll, and rice pudding. Occasionally in the afternoon, young Italo-Canadian girls from the neighbourhood dropped in for coffee after shopping at Maxie's Discount Drugs.

Behind the bar, beneath the TV that, like God, looked down on all, eyes always open, stood Pete, the owner, a man of sixty with a sad, wise face. A gentle, tough man. I once saw him wrestle an unruly customer down to the banquette and pin him there until the guy calmed down and took back the threats he'd leveled at another customer.

The waitress was Cynthia—maybe thirty and looking like she'd seen a thing or two in her time—also sad and wise and gentle and tough. Slender as a cigarette, maybe because of them, with huge, pale eyes reflecting almost all the light that entered them, a quick, warm smile and a lot of curls. Beautiful as an angel to anyone willing to stop a moment and gaze upon the wiry beauty of bargirls.

The Terminal was well-lit, always bright, almost cheerful. You had to look around for the darkness, but it was there.

I was too early. It was only 8:15. So after glancing in the window, I walked from the Terminal along the busy Danforth, past the parking lot and into Maxie's, where I took another look at sex aids and decided on a tube of greaseless jelly.

Back at the Terminal, shaky with nerves and all of a sudden sure that I'd never see Matthew again, I sat in a back booth, asked Cynthia for a Carlsberg, took out my criminology textbook and tried to read it. I had to force myself not to look up at the slightest movement of everyone in the bar.

After only a little while, I heard someone say, "Hi-hi." Absurdly, I thought, "Wow, but that guy's voice sounds a lot like Matthew's..."

I allowed myself to look up from my book, and there he was: lively and handsome and obviously thrilled that I was there. Through my mind jumped the thought that maybe he had thought he might never see me again.

The deal had been that we'd meet between 8:30 and 9:30. I looked at my watch. It was 8:35.

In his hand he held a wrapped bottle of wine, but he sat down and ordered a beer. Then we decided we'd better move across the aisle over to a no-smoking booth.

He looked around the place and had a good laugh. Not what he was used to, that seemed clear. Both of us dug in our pockets for quarters for the box and spent a bit of warm-up time flipping through the not-so-hot selections. I was nervous and talked too much, too stiffly. He didn't seem to notice, and before long, the problem was gone.

"Did you eat?" he asked. I'd been so nervous, excited, I'd had nothing all day but one bagel. He scolded me and told me I'd better order, and when I told him all I felt like eating was French fries, he scolded me again.

I told him the teacher had given me back my essay. "Oh, yes," he said, "I forgot to ask." He took the essay from me and carefully studied the teacher's comments. I thought his own comments smart and sweet.

I asked him how his day had gone, and he told me a bit about the video they were working on, saying that the men at the studio were amazed to see him there at eight a.m. but that it was okay after all.

We talked and drank beer and ate French fries and laughed and were both very happy that each other had turned up at the Terminal.

After a while, I led him back to my place.

But first, he paid the bill.

CHAPTER SIX

He'd been to Lovecraft and delighted in telling me about all the things he'd seen there. There wasn't the least hint of vulgarity in his descriptions and, as usual, no profanity in his speech. He showed me what he'd bought for our impending night: lambskin. And I showed him what I'd bought.

He uncorked the excellent wine he'd brought, and we took it to bed with us.

There followed what may have been hours of tender and passionate lovemaking—joyous lovemaking and professions of deep mutual admiration and laughing and touching and wine-drinking and cigarettes—for Matthew was extremely addicted to nicotine.

But despite the satisfying sensuality of our prolonged encounter with its numerous ecstatic climaxes, there was no intercourse, for Matthew was just too big.

At the end, he looked at the opened packages and the unrolled but unused safes and he laughed and said, "This is quite a spread we've got here—"

We both giggled, but he went on, "All our precautions have come to nothing …"

My heart fell a little, because I knew he had to be dissatisfied. "Yes," I answered.

"Well," he replied, "we certainly make a pair of interesting lovers."

Really, we did, but I hesitated before asking, "What do we do about that?" knowing it was silly to expect an answer. Even had our sex burned through the basement floor to Toronto bedrock, he'd be gone in a couple of days and I'd be back to being forty and brave in my cheerfulness.

"Nothing," he answered. But there was a sweetness in his voice, a surprising reassurance, and I knew that it meant he was not dissatisfied, that he'd enjoyed the things we'd done. I smiled from the inside out, and leaned across his reclining body to turn out the lamp.

As we lay in the gentle darkness, touching all along our sides, he sighed, "I'm falling in love ...."

But I didn't allow myself to respond to this in any way, not even by the slightest movement of my body because I know that men sometimes say such things in the passionate night, then wake to regret that they've been rash.

In the morning, we laughingly, lovingly, had our "interesting" sex again. And again. Each time, Matthew's largesse seemed less of a problem. Until it wasn't a problem at all.

He talked and talked that morning and I listened and learned the connection between the words rapt and rapture, for I could have looked at his handsome face and listened to his words forever. He told me about music and musicians, about the music business and about his family.

But on this morning, he suddenly grew extremely quiet, and lay very still as I sat beside him on the stretched-out futon. "I'm having an anxiety attack," he said softly, and he seemed to draw into himself, struggling with something that left him with a tense immobility different from sleep.

"Do you want me to leave you alone?" I whispered, thinking this anxiety might have something to do with his statement of the night before about falling in love. But he said no. He may even have asked me to hold him, for as our days together progressed, he often sought the false security of my helpless embrace.

I felt enormously sorry for him and wished there was something I could do to help him. I wasn't at all surprised that he should be this frightened, but I didn't ask myself why I wasn't surprised.

After a while, it passed and he said he was all right. It was time for me to go to work, and he said he'd come with me to the subway. He said he needed to walk.

I was early and asked him whether it was all right if I walked with him for a while, almost expecting him to say that he preferred to walk alone. But he didn't say that. He said, "Oh, yes ...."

Though it was only March, the weather was warm and sunny, a caressing spring morning. He mentioned how lucky we were with respect to the weather. He said his time in Toronto had been so nice that he was loath to leave.

He said, too, that, once before, when he'd been visiting a musician in Montana with the band, he'd had an anxiety attack because it was such a wonderful visit that he couldn't stand the thought of leaving the good times and the warmth behind. We talked about a traveler leaving the road, and he spoke like a man who'd been on the road a long time and was tired of it, but not tired enough to leave.

We got to the subway, and he kissed me—not as passionately as I had hoped—and presumably continued his walk in my neighbourhood as I went off to work. We'd agreed that he would phone me later.

Before we'd left that morning, two things had happened that involved the telephone. One was that my girlfriend had called to say she'd asked her friend about Matthew and had gotten no result. Her friend just had never heard of him. But he did say that nothing Matthew said sounded impossible—or even far-fetched.

The other thing was that when I was coming out of the shower, I heard Matthew talking. I assumed he was calling someone about the video and I was a tiny bit offended because he hadn't asked to use the phone. It only occurred to me to be offended because he had been so excruciatingly polite about everything else that this seemed a breach in otherwise impeccable manners.

But when I stepped into the room where he was, Matthew was nowhere near the phone.

That evening he called to say he'd be tied up with the video crew until late, but he wanted to know if I'd meet him at the Terminal at 10 p.m. He asked me to buy some wine and promised to reimburse me for it.

At ten I was waiting. I looked up to see Matthew coming toward me with a wide smile on his face and a dozen long-stemmed red roses in his hand.

I smiled widely myself.

But almost immediately he began a conversation that sounded very much like goodbye.

I could deal with that. Though disappointed, I said, "When you go I'll miss you."

He smiled, shrugged, looked down at the green marble slab between us and generally acted like a man who didn't want any trouble. A nice man, who, nevertheless, didn't want to take anything from a woman he was about to ditch.

I was so surprised and hurt that I couldn't hide it. Though we both made a valiant attempt at small talk, our conversation was stupidly awkward and I had to try hard to keep from crying because I was so insulted and humiliated. Matthew was getting angry. It was the first time I'd seen him exhibit any negative emotion at all, and, like everything else about him, even his anger seemed gentle, restrained, almost at times, an effort.

"Is this going to be a downer?" he asked in irritation, and I shook my head, unable to answer.

"Maybe I should just go?"

It was a good idea, actually, but not one I was going to jump to agree to. I just wasn't as strong as that, much as everything in me said it was the best thing that could happen. I didn't say anything.

"Look," Matthew said, conciliatory, "let's just spend one more night together."

The song "One More Night" started ringing through my head. I guess I agreed; I guess I said okay when he suggested we go back to my place, when he asked me yet again if he could be my guest.

We left the Terminal. I was so upset I kept dropping things—first the paper from the roses, which Matthew gracefully stooped to sweep up off the floor before heading for the cash and paying our bill.

Then I kept dropping roses. I just couldn't seem to keep a grip on them. Matthew was getting more and more angry, and when we reached my place, he snapped at me about some small thing I said.

Rather than being hurt, I felt relieved. As if the tremendous strain we'd been under—the strain of Matthew's gentle niceness—was finally being broken.

I tried to find a vase for the roses but couldn't. With shaky, angry motions, I shoved half of them into the wine bottle from the night before and the other half into a tall coffee mug. I had never treated roses so cavalierly.

"Let's have some wine," Matthew suggested, pouring us some. As we had the night before, we had to use coffee mugs for that because I'd never unpacked my wine glasses in the six months I'd lived in my place. He handed me a mug, then led me to our two hard-backed chairs where we sat facing each other kitty-corner as we had done before.

And I broke down.

I told him I was sorry to be so out of control but that knowing him had been a lovely holiday from my ordinary life. Now, I said, I realized the time had come to get back to it, and that was why I was so disappointed at the prospect of not seeing him again.

He said we could be friends, and I told him I didn't need any more friends.

He was really very nice, very kind. I knew he was trying to end things in a gentlemanly way, and I knew it was a very good idea to do so and I wanted it, too. The beautiful unreality of our being together was already consuming a tiring amount of energy. He would soon leave town and I would soon be back to making the most of life with the stolid nobility of one who had been taught that she was responsible for her own happiness.

I was tearful. He was tender. He suggested we should lie down together, and before we did, he said, "I was wondering whether I should tell you this, but I'm beginning to fall in love with you—"

I found this comment a little strange, considering his breathed declaration of the night before. But I answered truthfully that I was falling a little in love with him, too, and that was the problem. It made perfect sense to both of us that that was an excellent reason never to see each other again.

CHAPTER SEVEN

We lay beside each other in the light from the small lamp and he said, "You are a survivor. You don't need anybody to take care of you. A man needs a woman he can work for. He needs to know that when he's doing a job he doesn't want to do—when he's out on the road and it seems like it's never going to end—he can say to himself, 'I have to keep doing this. I have to do this for her'. You don't need that."

Again I began to weep. "So," I said, "what's supposed to happen to people like me?"

"What?"

"Do I have to spend my whole life alone and without anybody to take care of me just because I seem strong?" I felt the old familiar loneliness scratch its slogan on the wall of my chest. "It's so unfair. People like me need somebody to take care of them, too …."

Something seemed to snap in Matthew. A sudden intensity made him rigid. He compelled me to turn my eyes toward his, which were blazing with a dark light that seemed to come from the night itself. "I'll take care of you," he swore. "I'll take care of you for the rest of your life. You'll never have to worry about anything again. I'll take you home with me to Hartford. You can live in my house."

It was hard to look at him. I smiled. I had to smile. "You'll regret saying this," I warned him. "In the morning you'll be very, very sorry. You'll wish you'd never—"

"No," he swore, staring at me like a hypnotist. "I would have at nineteen, but not at thirty-five. I'll take care of you. You have touched my heart."

In my experience, men seldom talked about their hearts unless certain barriers had been let to fall. I turned out the lamp and snuggled beside Matthew, suddenly totally exhausted. I didn't know what to think. I wished that it were true that Matthew would take care of me. I had never met anyone like him and I wondered if that meant that, unlike all the others I had met, he really could take care of me as they could not.

Out of the smooth darkness I heard Matthew's voice. "Goodnight, my love," he said.

I had known him for fifty-six hours.

In the morning, it didn't even occur to me to wonder whether the charged conversation of the night before would alter our behaviour toward each other.

We were as happy, passionate, tender and talkative as ever. In fact, as I came out of the shower, I again heard Matthew carrying on a conversation. Quickly, I moved toward the door to see whether he was using the phone.

But I was soaking wet and it took me a moment to towel myself before I could step out of the washroom and onto the rug that led to the other room.

Matthew was sitting in a chair across the room from the phone leafing through a book of my poems.

After I dressed, we left, and for the first time, he took the subway with me, getting off before me at the Bay station, which made sense because the studio he said he was working at was in Yorkville. On the subway, he sat very close to me, and when it was time for him to get off, he promised to call at 7:30, and he tenderly said goodbye. As the subway pulled out of the station, he turned and smiled at me and waved.

It occurred to me that I had now known Matthew for Sunday, Monday and Tuesday and that he had not changed his clothes. In fact, he had borrowed a large shirt from me one day to wear under the panther sweater, carefully leaving his own shirt over a chair at my place.

He spoke so often of his preference for designer clothes that when I got home, out of curiosity, I checked the label of his shirt. It was Fruit of the Loom, and the shirt was very old.

But when Matthew called at 7:30, I was as always thrilled to hear his voice, and he seemed thrilled when I said that of course I'd be delighted to meet him at the Terminal in a little while. He said he had a bit of business to do and asked me if I wanted to come along. I said of course. Partly because I wanted to be where he was and partly because I was longing for some kind—any kind—of verification of all he'd been telling me about Neil Young and about his own marvellous and long-standing career.

He said the job was to take a signed album from Young to the manager of a pub not far from my place and to chat the manager up as a public relations job for a very prominent Toronto promoter whom Matthew had talked about over and over in our conversations. I was dying to meet someone who knew Matthew from business—someone who knew him at all.

As usual, I met him at the Terminal. By now, the waitress, Cynthia, and the owner were starting to be very friendly, were treating us not only as regulars, but as a couple.

We listened to the jukebox for a while. Matthew showed me the signed album. I couldn't read a word of the inscription. It was very scribbly. I felt a chill come over me because something told me it was not Neil Young who'd signed the album, but Matthew himself.

I had, though, no reason to think such a thing. And even as I was thinking it, Matthew handed me a gift elaborately wrapped in black paper with a silver ribbon. I told him black and silver were my favourites as I opened the package to reveal Swiss chocolates from Eaton's. I thought it was a very elegant gift.

I told Matthew I had a present for him, too—real coffee to replace the instant we'd been drinking. We both laughed, finished our beers and hopped in a cab to head for the pub where Matthew was to meet the manager.

The Highlander was not like the Terminal. It was new, trendy, built only a few years before, dark in every respect and crowded with young quasi-Yuppies. Compared to it, the noise-level at the Terminal resembled a church.

The minute we stepped in the door, we were met by a bouncer. Matthew immediately handed him the album and asked him, "Please give this to the manager." As the man disappeared into the crowd, I noticed that Matthew was nervous again with the peculiar shakiness he'd shown the day we'd first walked out of the "wake" together.

But we found a seat at the bar and almost at once began to talk to a few others there. It was easy to see that, though the dour blonde female bartender was no Cynthia, the Highlander was as much a neighbourhood bar as the Terminal—or as any in Toronto for that matter.

After a while, the people we were talking to drifted away and Matthew started to tell me about his wonderful house and all the things it contained: paintings, china, a pinball machine, two pianos—one a Bösendorfer, a priceless gift from Neil Young. He painstakingly retold the details of the night—his birthday—he'd received this wonderful surprise. He told me that no one but him was ever allowed to touch this piano. Then he thought for a moment and said that now he would have to put a chair in that room so I could sit and listen to him play.

And I, perched on a stool in the dim, noisy, trendy bar in Toronto, with forty years behind me and God knew what before me, loved—as a child loves a slithery bubble that skips away from its breath—the image of myself sitting beside Matthew listening to his smoky, hurt voice singing for me alone.

He told me more about the house, the neighbours. I listened. He turned to me, and for the first time said, "I love you." And of course I said, "I love you, too."

CHAPTER EIGHT

He bought what seemed like a lot of drinks. Beer for me, beers for others at the bar—who reciprocated—scotch for himself, though he had told me scotch had got him in trouble before and that he made a point of staying away from it.

He handed me a thick wad of bills and told me to put it in my purse and hang on to it for him. A little later, he asked me to peel off one of the outside bills—a twenty—so he could pay for yet more drinks.

In a little while, out of the smoky, noisy, semi-darkness came the manager. He shook Matthew's hand, obviously very glad to see him, and they commenced a long conversation of which I could hear nothing except the introduction of myself. I also heard Matthew offer the manager a drink, heard the manager say he wasn't supposed to imbibe on duty, heard Matthew order a drink and a cup of coffee, saw the manager pour the drink into the coffee and take a few big gulps. Matthew looked like a man who knew exactly what to do every step of the way—smooth, friendly, in control, impressive. Professional.

And I assumed his profession was the one he said it was. The fact that the pub manager was nervous as a pup the whole time and seemed tremendously deferential to boot only made Matthew—who wasn't losing his cool for a second—all the more impressive.

But hard as I tried, I couldn't hear any of the business talk between the two men, except for one fragmented sentence concerning the promoter. "When he called me and told me the person coming was ..." the manager said, slightly mispronouncing Matthew's name, "I ..."

The rest was lost as the manager turned away to say something to someone else. Matthew leaned toward me and said, "They always do that—say my name wrong."

The comment struck me as very odd. Matthew's last name was extremely simple. Odder still was how Matthew had a preternatural ability to jump in with an explanation at the precise moment a question entered my mind. He was a skilled mind-reader and only he knew why.

The evening ended almost at closing time with a game of pinball in the basement room of the pub. Only Matthew and I and the manager were left down there.

When Matthew had told me about his own pinball machine, I'd told him how I loved the game and how I sometimes played in the street arcades.

The three-way challenge was a delicate manoeuvering of winning and losing between the men. Matthew played very well and I, of course, was not as good as the men but not bad enough to embarrass my date or his associate. In short, I was exactly right. And so was Matthew. He played a brilliant first game, then let the manager win, then won again.

When the manager again disappeared into his office, telling us not to go yet, seeming to want to draw out the evening as long as possible, Matthew bent his face toward mine and whispered, "I love you. Do you love me?"

"Yes," I said trying not to show any hesitation.

"Are you sure?"

I couldn't answer. Without any anger or disappointment—but no snideness or sarcasm, either, he said, "I guess you're not."

When we left the Highlander, it was raining, and Matthew became impatient with the city and the night because it took so long to get a cab. But once we finally got one, all anger fled from him. He seemed to have no energy for anger, as if he'd abandoned that emotion a long time ago—or never got it right in the first place. There was a detachment to him in moments in which anger would have been appropriate—even when it was present—that was surprising in a person who could be so passionate in his professions of love and his expressions of delight over how good and how at ease he felt when he was with me.

"Incredible!" he would say over and over again. About knowing me. About his comfort in my presence. About my body. About my mind. "Incredible!" "Incredible!"

When we got back to my place from the Highlander, I handed Matthew a large white bag the manager had given him and which he'd asked me to hold.

"No," Matthew said, "that's yours—"

I opened the bag to find a big, soft, very expensive-looking pale yellow sweatshirt with the name of the pub and its symbol discretely embroidered in black on the front.

Delighted, I immediately put it on.

"Are you sure you don't want it yourself?"

"No. We get so many T-shirts and sweatshirts given to us you wouldn't believe it …."

I believed it. Like all the other details Matthew had off-handedly tossed at me about his work and the lifestyle that went with it, this seemed dead on.

He rhapsodized about how wonderful I looked in the sweatshirt. In fact, we immediately fell into bed and locked in an embrace.

But in what seemed a matter of seconds, Matthew was sound asleep on top of me.

Never in all my life had I seen a person fall so quickly and so deeply into sleep. It was totally impossible to wake him. He was gone. I had no choice but to go to sleep under him. I couldn't even move to turn out the lamp.

Finally, after some time, I woke to find him rolling off me. I took off the sweatshirt, turned out the light and slept.

In the morning I awoke to thoughts of how I might begin to dismantle my life in order to move to Hartford.

It was Thursday, and before work, Matthew walked me a long few blocks to my bank. I had told him that the next day I was leaving to visit my brother in Utica, New York. Something about this seemed to bother him, and not sure what, I thought maybe he'd miss me, so I told him he was welcome to come with me if he liked.

I told him I'd arranged to take the next day off work to be with him as long as possible before my bus left at two in the afternoon, and I told him, too, I'd take the latest bus possible because, according to what he'd originally told me, the Sunday I got back was supposed to be Matthew's last day in town.

He said he'd think about going with me, but he seemed remarkably nonchalant for a man who'd declared his love and might have only a few hours left with his beloved.

Come to think of it, I was pretty nonchalant myself.

As we walked to the bank, Matthew talked again about his brothers, especially the one who was now successful in some aspect of the arts—exactly what his brother did was unclear to me. Matthew mentioned, as he had before, that when he was twenty-one, he'd been hit by a car in Yorkville, an accident that resulted in a semicircular scar between his right eyebrow and his nose, another scar under his jaw and scars on his body he said he had, but which I never saw. He said, too, that this accident had resulted in his inability to have children and that in compensation for that, there'd been a very large settlement.

He said he wanted to use the money to get state-of-the-art equipment for his musical career, but that his brother had wanted to borrow it for something else. They'd quarreled and never really mended the breach.

When we got to the bank, Matthew came inside and took a chair while I did my business. I knew the manager and had a friendly chat with him, which Matthew commented on pleasantly later.

We left the bank, and, having a few minutes before it was time for me to get on the subway, went across the street to a tarted-up greasy spoon with flocked wallpaper for a coffee.

Matthew told me I'd been wonderful at the Highlander the night before. He said my behaviour had been perfect for his business purposes. He said he was proud of me.

I told him I thought he'd been pretty impressive himself. He had, I said, the perfect combination of arrogance and humility. We both laughed. Then he told me a story of an evening he'd spent with a famous musician who'd taken a crowd of people to a restaurant and after dinner ordered a whole bottle of cognac for each guest. Matthew had been appalled and disgusted. He very often mentioned his distaste for excess of any kind, and he seemed to have found this incident really disturbing.

What I found really disturbing was the way he suddenly seemed to lose interest in the conversation, seemed to be studying something—or someone—over my shoulder and reacting nervously to it, or him or her ....

Suddenly he seemed in a hurry and anxious to leave the restaurant. Though he said nothing, I quickly finished my coffee. I offered to pay the small bill, but he refused and paid the bill himself.

We got on the subway, but instead of getting off at Bay, near the studio, Matthew got off one stop before. I thought this a little strange, but thought that perhaps he was headed south to finally go to the apartment he was supposed to be minding to change his clothes. Only his underwear had been changed since I'd met him. I was now lending him my shirt and washing his.

As usual, he told me he'd call me later. As usual, he turned and smiled and waved as the train pulled out of the station with me on it on my way to work.

It was growing very difficult for me to concentrate on my job. Only one woman there was in any way a friend, and after work that day, I had a coffee with her and told her all about Matthew—not only the good things, but also the gnawing doubts about all the music business names he was always dropping, about his descriptions of his work and his career, about the fact I couldn't find his name on any record anywhere nor locate anybody who'd ever heard of him.

As it happened, this woman had had experience in the music business herself, and she said that, while some of what

Matthew said seemed a little odd, all of it was certainly possible.

Once more I was left with the feeling that to question Matthew might be to insult him in a way he did not deserve.

CHAPTER NINE

THE EMOTIONAL PACE OF the days was exhausting.

I got home and soon after Matthew called to say he'd be tied up for a while with the guys working on the video but that I should meet him at the Terminal at ten.

It never bothered me that he always wanted to meet me so late. I needed time to myself, since when I was with him, the being with demanded all my time and energy. Plus I figured that, in his profession, ten p.m. was early. It amazed me that he could get away so early every night and that he preferred to spend the time with me rather than drinking and taking drugs with his buddies, which was what I assumed recording artists preferred to do.

But he told me that some musicians had nothing to do with drugs and that he was one of them. Though, he said, he sometimes thought he was still too much into alcohol.

I took a nap, so tired that I seemed to sleep as deeply as Matthew could. But I awoke in plenty of time to get to the Terminal at ten.

Except that as I was about to leave, the phone rang. The call was from a girlfriend in some distress over the impending separation of her and the man she'd lived with for a couple of years, so I had no choice but to listen and to sympathize. When I hung up and looked at my watch, I knew I might not make it to the Terminal exactly at ten, but sometimes Matthew had been a little late, so I didn't think he'd notice.

I rushed over. Through the window I could see that instead of sitting in a booth, Matthew was perched on a stool at the bar. Cynthia was beside him and Pete, the owner, was standing in front of him. They were trying to console him because he was so nervous that I hadn't shown up earlier.

"Here she is," Cynthia laughed when I walked in. She got me a beer and George went off to make us a couple of plates of French fries.

The minute they'd stepped a little distance away, Matthew began to frantically declare how much he loved me—agitatedly, eagerly, and with, I thought, no real reason to be so excited.

"I'm so in love with you," he said, his eyes shining like fire reflected in black marble, "I can't believe it. I'm so in love, so in love."

I felt the urgent need to calm him down. I told him with laughing gentleness that I loved him too. On the bar was a gift wrapped in black paper with a bow made of silver spikes. "What's this?" I asked, teasing.

He handed it to me but told me not to open it until we got home.

He couldn't seem to stop touching me. The stools we sat on were close, with only a small space between, which he filled with his hands, reaching for as much of me as he could touch without the few others in the bar thinking us vulgar.

I was slightly embarrassed at his hunger, as if he had to touch me regardless of what the others thought—but it seemed a sweet hunger, a sweet anxiety that only I could—and did—calm with touches and kisses and reassurances as if I were offering to a beautiful child some promise to keep him still until night.

The French fries came, slathered in gravy as always and accompanied by more beer. Laughing, we ate them, watching Pete's TV suspended over the bar.

Once more, Matthew began to talk about his wonderful house in the States. About how there were two acres of land. About how a retired U.S. general lived next door. About how the general liked to think he was keeping an eye on Matthew's place when Matthew was on the road, but that the general wasn't crazy about the two gay painters who lived there in his absence and who were the ones really keeping an eye on the place.

He talked with animation, as if this house were splendid, but it sounded happily chaotic, too, full of art treasures he'd gathered in his extensive travels, but also full of the sloppy memorabilia that a musician brings back from the road. I imagined Matthew as a man of many and varied possessions.

And he imagined that someday soon I might become one of them. As I listened to him talk about his home, he turned to me, the low fires keeping vigil in his eyes, and he said, "Will you marry me?"

I laughed and said yes.

He told me I could have a little room of my own for my writing. He said I wouldn't have to work again. He said, "I make …" but his voice trailed off before he named a figure. He was, this night, more handsome than ever, his lean, pale, strong-boned face agile with emotion, his mouth soft with sudden smiles and compulsive kisses, his thick black curls dancing in the blue light of the Terminal TV.

I asked him if he'd thought about coming with me to Utica, and he said, "Well, I've thought about it. I spoke to the guys. They can spare me some of the time—I've cleared Saturday, but Sunday still looks iffy …."

I wasn't disappointed—or hopeful either. The thought of bringing Matthew to meet my brother seemed to feel the same way a dream feels when you have something in it that would make your real life so much better, but you know you can't drag it back up with you into the reality of day.

"This weekend could cost me four thousand dollars," he said, glancing over at me from the side of his eye.

"Oh, well, then," I said, a tiny bit relieved, "you'd better forget about it …."

"We'll see," he answered.

As we watched TV, Michelle Phillips came on, and he seemed spellbound by her, staring intently at the screen and asking me not to talk while she was on. I found this very odd, but very pleasantly requested, so I, too, looked at the screen.

To watch television with him, to talk about his house—which he had suddenly begun to refer to as "our house," to sit beside him laughing and touching, was such happiness, such ordinary happiness, that I wished with all my heart that the two of us might enjoy these simple pleasures forever.

After a while, we decided that if I was very discreet, I could open my gift. I held it down between our two bar stools and removed the spiky bow and the dark paper. Wrapped in tissue in a box from Eaton's was a pair of black panties edged in black lace.

Matthew, as was his habit, asked me if we could spend the night together.

Of course, I said yes.

"But first," I said, "there's something that's bothering me—"

"What's that?" he asked, a little nervous.

He still had not changed his clothes. It looked as though he'd been nowhere but at work or with me since the minute we'd met.

"The cockatiel. Who's feeding it? Who's giving it water? You said on Sunday that you were looking after it. Now it's Thursday. Is it dangling from its perch somewhere or something?"

"Oh, no," Matthew smiled. "I gave the keys to the apartment to one of the technicians. I had him run over and take care of it."

I smiled, relieved. It didn't occur to me to ask him why he hadn't told the technician to bring him back a clean shirt.

He paid Pete, peeling twenties off his wad again and declaring that he couldn't believe how small the tab was—as if he were used to much more expensive places.

I found that a tiny bit embarrassing, but Pete didn't seem to mind. He liked Matthew. And when I was with Matthew, he also liked me. Everybody seemed to like us.

We were golden, as golden as the beer we kept downing.

CHAPTER TEN

For the past couple of days, I had been complaining about a sliver in my finger—a sliver that may have been part of the thorn of a rose. Matthew became my surgeon.

As we came to my place, it was hurting and I mentioned it. I had told him before that I had had other friends who were pianists and that it was my experience that pianists had very strong hands.

We stepped inside, and before he'd removed his dark coat, he said, "Would you like me—with my pianist's hands—to take care of that sliver for you?"

I nodded yes and held out my hand.

He took it gently, but squeezed very hard. I kept my eyes on his darkly intense, handsome face. Though what he was doing should have hurt a great deal, I remember no pain. He seemed quite afraid of hurting me, though, and I had to encourage him to keep at the sliver.

"You're not hurting me—really, you're not ..."

His fiery eyes flashed sidewise into mine and he swore, "I don't ever want to hurt you."

He succeeded in removing the sliver and told me it was a good thing because he could tell it was beginning to be infected. We joked about his saving my life and he said that now he was like Androcles, who'd taken the thorn from the foot of the lion.

"Like him," I said, "I am now indebted to you for life."

Matthew said nothing in reply.

In the morning, as usual, we loved again. We had coffee, which we took turns making, at Matthew's insistence. We talked and talked, and the hours flew as fast as a junkie's cash.

I packed for my trip. Though we made some contingency plans, it was clear that Matthew wasn't coming along. I thought it odd that he had to work this Sunday but had been free enough to spend the whole afternoon at the wake and the whole evening with me the previous Sunday, but I didn't question him. Nor was I very disappointed. He couldn't come and that was fine. I gave him my brother's phone number.

Though my bus wasn't until two, we set out for the bus terminal at about noon. As we walked to the subway, I mentioned how ironic it was that I should now know the man who had written a song that—every other time I had visited—my brother had sung for me. Matthew said that of course, he'd not written the song for guitar, which my brother played, but piano. He mentioned some technical details about writing in this key or that.

Matthew came all the way to the bus terminal with me. I wondered how he could do that without telling anybody at the studio that he would be late. He never seemed to go near the telephone at my place.

As we neared the terminal, he seemed a little nervous. He told me that he was very bad at goodbyes. He said he'd take me to the terminal coffee shop and that I could order myself some lunch, but that after I ordered, he would just disappear.

I asked him, instead, to stand in line with me while I bought my ticket. "Then," I said, "you can take off."

All the time I'd been with Matthew, I had never seen him with any possessions except cash. No wallet. No ID. No keys. The night before, he'd mentioned keys in connection with the cockatiel, but I never saw them. And I never heard them, either, though there were many times I heard him take off his coat and his pants.

But he had keys now.

Because before we left for the bus terminal, I had given him my keys—an extra set to my place. He had not asked for these keys—nor ever mentioned staying at my place when I was away, but something compelled me to give him the keys. I had told this man that I loved him. I had said yes to his offers of marriage. I had trusted him with my heart—and the rest of my body, too.

But the real something that made me give him the keys was a feeling I would not allow myself to admit, though I knew I had it—the deep, certain, instinctive fear that without those keys, Matthew would have no place to sleep.

I bought my ticket. We said goodbye. It was a very shaky parting on Matthew's part. He seemed scared—more scared than loving. My last words to him were, "Don't worry about anything." I don't know what I thought he might have to worry about.

Before he left me, he waited for me to put my wallet back in my purse. He seemed to study the purse, and he commented on the fact that it was as organized as the rest of me—very organized. "You sure have a lot of compartments in that thing," he said.

We hugged. Some men feel solid when you hug them, like you're holding on. Others feel fragile, like you're holding them together. Mostly, Matthew felt like that.

He moved away. He said something I couldn't catch, but I didn't want to spoil the moment by asking him to repeat it. His smile as he said it was casual.

I turned and headed for the door to the platform. But instinct told me to turn around. Matthew was staring at me, raising his hand to wave goodbye.

CHAPTER ELEVEN

THE FIRST THING I learned when I got to my brother's was that the book from which he'd learned "Matthew's" song credited it to someone else.

We called all my brother's friends who knew about this type of music, but nobody was home. The date of the song was exactly the year Matthew had said he'd written it, but the name on it was definitely somebody else's. My brother and I came to the uneasy conclusion that perhaps the credit had been mistakenly given, as sometimes does happen. But we came to the even uneasier conclusion that Matthew had lied about the song—and if about that—what else?

And he had the keys to my place!

It was a very distressing forty-eight hours. I was totally preoccupied with who or what this man was or wasn't.

My original plan had been to take a bus back on Sunday that would arrive in Toronto at midnight. Matthew was planning to meet that bus.

Instead, I took an earlier bus so that I could go back to my place and prepare myself for what I thought was the most likely scenario—that I had seen the last of my Black Irish, my strange songster, my demon. It is hundreds of miles from Utica, New York to Toronto, Ontario. For part of them I worried, for part, I prayed. For a few minutes—on the border—I wept. Mostly I sat immobile, stunned at my own desperate weakness.

I had known Matthew for exactly one week. But it seemed as if I'd known him forever.

By the time I got to Toronto, I was a wreck. Somehow I made it from the bus terminal home.

As soon as I got in, I could see that he'd been there. The bed was made—but not in my usual way. There were matches and a few coins on the dresser that hadn't been there when we'd left.

But little else seemed disturbed. As I looked around, though, I noticed a couple of things—that someone had used the phone, that someone had apparently gone through a file of my income tax papers that I'd left lying on top of my desk. Whoever had gone through the papers had left out a T-form from my bank that had on it my name and address and also, of course, the number of the account and the amount of interest it had accrued during the previous year.

Two drawers containing papers and odds and ends showed definite signs of having been rifled through.

And in the sink was a single coffee mug with a lipstick stain on it.

I panicked, sure Matthew had slept in my apartment with another woman and sure he had been looking for some paper that would allow him to steal from me in some clever, complicated way.

Frantic, I pulled the sheets from the bed and stuck them in the washer. I called Ruth, my girlfriend, and also my brother—both of whom could hear the terror in my voice and each of whom tried to calm me down, assuring me that it was quite possible that there were other explanations for what I'd found. To them, the evidence that Matthew had done something wrong seemed slight.

But still, Ruth offered to remove my valuables to her place and to let me stay there for the night, and she agreed to come with me to the bus terminal in case Matthew should, in fact, show up. All three of us seemed quite convinced that he would not.

I finished the wash and put the sheets back on the bed. I threw away the roses Matthew had given me. Of course, they were dead now, anyway. I threw out the black paper and the spiky bow. I tossed the bottle from the rare wine.

But when it came to the yellow sweatshirt and the black lace panties—I couldn't. I took a better look at the panties, which I had thought were silk and saw that they were not. But still, they were very fine and the label said they'd been made in France.

In the hours in which I sat there waiting for my girlfriend to pick me up, I felt first paralyzing fear, then self-disgust, then something I didn't realize would be more long-lasting than fear or disgust. I felt that Matthew was gone and that I would miss him for a good long time.

During the course of these hours, my landlady came down and told me she'd had a bad scare when she'd seen a man leave my apartment. I'd totally forgotten to tell her that there'd be somebody there while I was away—only that I'd be gone myself.

As I apologized, she said that the man had appeared to be dazed because, he claimed, he'd just bumped his head. She said he'd been alone as far as she knew and that he'd been very quiet.

The hours slowly crawled away and finally Ruth came and we took off, headed downtown to meet—or not to meet—Matthew.

We got there before midnight, so we went into the terminal coffee shop. I was so nervous, I chattered compulsively about how I'd surely seen the last of my strange lover. It seems to me now that I never stopped to think why we were so very sure that that should be so.

Calmly, Ruth told me that should he not arrive, she'd do her best to get me through the night, but that if he did come, she'd check him out and if she didn't like what she saw, she'd demand the keys back from him and ask him to leave me alone.

"But on the other hand," she said, "if it looks like he's no axe murderer or anything and if he's obviously expecting a sweet romantic reunion, I'll drive the two of you home."

We sat perched on stools at the high, busy counter. A waiter who'd heard so many stories that not even mine would sound odd took our orders for coffee and tea. Around us the crowd ebbed and flowed. Between me and the door to the station lobby was the rack of refrigerated shelves holding the long day's remaining wedges of pie and pedestalled glasses of rice pudding. Partly through the dim glass windows of this unit and partly through plain air, I could see people coming and going in the lobby.

Dozens went by. Ruth and I watched the clock. Or rather, I watched the clock and she watched me.

It was not yet midnight when I looked up and saw Matthew—only the barest glimpse of him passing the door.

"He came!" I nearly shouted, hopping down from the stool and went dashing after him. I must have been remarkably quick, for he was only a few yards from the door when I caught him.

He turned. In the fluorescent light of the bus terminal lobby, the planes of his handsome face were harshly exaggerated, but he was smiling at me, and his hair shone like polished ebony.

He still had not changed his clothes.

With nervous haste, I explained that my girlfriend had come with me because I'd come into town early. Perhaps he seemed a little nervous, too, or annoyed at this news, but it was hardly noticeable. I led him into the coffee shop and made the introduction.

It seemed fine. Matthew's smooth, intelligent, lively talk was exactly right. He told me at once how he'd accidentally scared the landlady and how he couldn't even respond to her questions articulately because he'd been in a daze after bumping his head on the low door out of my place.

Ruth asked him about the video he was working on, and he began to answer, but then he skittered off the subject and on to the topic of her job. Since the video was now supposed to be done, I interrupted him to ask whether they'd finished. "The end of the month," he answered with cheerful offhandedness, "a couple more days ..."

We walked to Ruth's car, and she offered us a ride home. Matthew, learning that she worked for a film company, launched into such a shower of name-dropping that Ruth was quite stunned.

All the way back to my place, his deep, smooth voice went on and on about the people he knew where she worked, the experiences he'd had at various studios ...

It wasn't arrogant, just aggressive—nervous—as one might be when trying to impress the best friend of a beloved.

When we got home, Matthew lost his slickness. We sat facing each other, and he, laughing and boyish, asked me whether my brother had told me to "slow down, you're going too fast …" quoting the old sixties song.

I didn't really answer, and he launched into a little speech about how all his friends were warning him that he had taken a very long time to get over his failed first marriage and that he should be more careful about me.

"What friends? Where do they live? When did you speak with them?" I wanted to ask. But I didn't.

I showed him presents I'd brought to him from my brother, a bookseller. The first was a beautiful calendar about angling. Matthew turned the coloured pages over one by one and said, "Oh, this is for people who fly-fish …" in an odd tone of voice, just as if he'd never spent a good deal of time on two separate occasions telling me how much he loved this sport.

My other gift for him was a big photo book of New England scenes. This he smiled at appreciatively, almost laughingly. "I know it's a bulky present to give somebody who has to carry their stuff home soon, but …"

He became agitated, childlike. "What do you mean carry home?" he demanded. "It sounds like you're not coming with me!" He reached for my hands as we sat there face to face.

"Matthew," I began, "I really care for you, but …"

But what?

Immediately, he jumped in to stop whatever it was I was going to say. "This sounds like confrontation politics," he said, shakily, as though he were scared.

"No!" I swore, uneasy at his growing distress. I stood and took his head in my hands, holding it against my stomach, a gesture of comfort that never failed to soothe men before. "No ..."

"Please," he said, standing and leading me toward the bed, "please. I want everything to be exactly the way it was before ..."

We lay down. Soon, Matthew was fast asleep. But I lay in the darkness beside him for a long time. It was as I lay there that I noticed how strange he smelled—there was a strong chemical odor emanating from him as though it were breathing out of the pores of his lean body.

Out of the pores of my own body seeped the sweat of fear.

But, as on every other night on which I'd lain with Matthew, fear gave way to the comfort of his body, hard and warm along the planes of my own, and I fell asleep.

Fell asleep with the sickening realization that I was going to somehow have to begin to reclaim my ordinary life.

CHAPTER TWELVE

The next morning we were as intimate as ever, in fact, more so.

But after we loved, I was again gripped with the terror that had rocked me to sleep the night before. Fearing Matthew might sense the subtle change in feeling between us, I casually mentioned that I was nervous, and when he said, "About what?" I answered, "About us …"

As he had often asked me, I now asked him to hold me tight.

And it occurred to me why a person afraid of cancer will light a cigarette to allay his fears, or a junkie jab himself with a needleful to get away from his terror of junk.

In a little while, we dressed and left my place. We had time, so I suggested we go out for a coffee. I was so shaky it was hard for me to hide it, and hard for me to talk.

"I'm sorry to be this way …"

"The problem is," Matthew answered with a patient smile, "the nervousness is catchy."

The comment made me try harder, and before long, our conversation was as natural and warm and friendly and funny as it had always been. As we left the coffee shop and headed for the subway, Matthew mentioned that he was afraid he'd bowled Ruth over by dropping too many names. I couldn't think of anything to say.

As if mention of show business stirred memories, he began to talk about his youth, and about his "one hit song." He told me again how it had affected his life, giving him a taste of fame that was irresistible. I asked him again how old he'd been when this happened, and he said—as he had before—"nineteen," which put the date at exactly what it was in the book my brother had showed me. I wanted to mention what I'd discovered about the song, but I wasn't ready for the sort of confrontation I thought would result.

Matthew said it had been a wonderful idea to go out for coffee, that it had relaxed us both. I smiled and we walked on together, very close.

We got into the subway, still chatting. I began to tell him about my love for Beethoven. When we got to Yonge and Bloor, he said, "I'd love to hear this—you are so animated. But the journey is far too short." With that he kissed me and stood to get off the train. We made plans to meet on campus after my class that night. I suggested an easy-to-reach street corner, but he said no. "I don't like standing around on corners."

Finally, we settled on a building at the university and a flexible range of times in case neither of us could get there exactly when planned. He smiled and waved and got off.

I couldn't suppress the worry that he got off at Yonge and Bloor every day not to walk to the studio but to switch to the southbound train, maybe to wander aimlessly around the Eaton Centre or some other mall.

I went to work. I went to school. I finished class. I waited. For an hour and fifteen minutes—with no sign of Matthew.

The rainy night turned cold and wild with ripping winds that battered the still-bare trees.

I waited so long that the building I was waiting in closed, though the kindly caretaker took pity on me and let me stand inside after he'd locked up.

Finally, I gave up. I walked out of the building and toward the street, balancing on the curb and leaning into the traffic looking for a cab. The wind blew so hard that my clothes stung my body as they flapped around me, and the rain was a frigid, continuous slap in the face.

I had not stood on the curb for more than a minute when I looked up to see a dark figure materialize out of the distance, running toward me, soaking wet, rain dripping from his coat, his eyes and hair blacker and more wild than the savage night.

I opened my arms instinctively and he ran into them as if that was where he'd been headed forever. "You've got to take care of me," he gasped. "I'm all drugged out …."

I clutched him, trying to pull him out of the driving rain and in under the flimsy shelter of my small umbrella. "Come on," I said, "I'll get us a cab."

"No," he insisted, "No. I want to get inside now. One of the buildings … one of the residences."

He seemed quite coherent, but he looked stranger than ever, so pale, so handsome, the black curls a tight wet tumble about his drawn face. He was helpless and childlike—lost, but also controlling, the way a skillful little boy is when he teeters on the verge of tantrum.

I was freezing, but not scared. I felt my only concern was to get him out of the rain. He, however, turned out to be very choosy about which building he wanted to be in. As we passed one after another, huddled tight together, he explained that it being the second to the last day of the video taping, the drug and sex dealers had arrived at the studio. He seemed to imply that he had no trouble passing up the "eighteen-year-olds," but that he had succumbed to peer pressure and bought and consumed a huge quantity of drugs. He said he was very stoned, though he wasn't acting what I considered out of control of himself.

At long last—both of us wet and freezing—we arrived at the building he'd been seeking.

It had an archway between two sections and set in the arch were the doors to each part. Matthew immediately went to the north door—the archway was brightly lit—and began yanking on it with a sort of almost-lazy anger. When the door refused to open, he began to pound on it. He seemed panicky, but, as always, there was a wall of some kind between him and his emotion, as if he didn't have the strength, the interest to be fully angry.

No one came to the door. Exasperated, he pulled me away from the door and leaned against the wall inside the front of the arch. From his pocket he pulled a handful of strange-looking things. He told me what they were, proudly, as if it were quite a coup for him to be in possession. But knowing nothing about drugs, I didn't know what he was talking about.

My pity for him was rapidly turning to disgust—and there was no wall between *me* and *my* negative emotions!

He said, "Go get me some papers and I'll smoke a joint to come down."

This really angered me. I was supposed to go out in the raging night to get him papers? I told him I didn't even know where one purchased such things.

He wrinkled his face in mild disdain at my ignorance. "Just go to a drugstore."

Sure. I wasn't just angry. I was also confused about a person being so stoned that they had to smoke to come down. I felt like saying, "Pardon my ignorance, Matthew, but I was under the impression people smoked to get high ..."

He was, of course, not very angry at my refusal to do as he bid. He looked away from me toward the door, and he saw what I saw—a man with a pizza ringing the doorbell. The door opened. The pizza man slipped in. And so did Matthew and I.

The building was one of the lovely neo-Gothic student residences that dot the campus of the University of Toronto. "This is where I went to school for a year ..." Matthew said. He had referred to the university a number of times, but I got the feeling his familiarity with the place was far more recent than the distant days of his education.

We moved confidently down a long, high-ceilinged corridor interrupted by heavy, dark wooden doors. Knowing exactly which door to open, Matthew led us into one of the lovely, stately, Victorian common rooms.

As soon as we entered, I saw why Matthew wanted us to be in this room. By the tall door stood a baby grand piano. The room was furnished like a sturdy sort of drawing room with a long couch before a fireplace in which a few logs glowed. Though a young man was fast asleep on this couch, Matthew proceeded at once to set the stage for a private concert.

Near the piano was a high-backed wing chair facing the fireplace. He struggled to turn the heavy thing around so that it faced the piano, and he gestured for me to sit down. Reluctantly, I did. From time to time, a person would open the door and look in on us, but, though I was afraid someone might throw us out, no one questioned us, or even seemed much interested at all.

When I was seated to his satisfaction, Matthew began to play. I was so stunned at this strange course of events, so angry—more with myself than with him—so disappointed, that I rested my head against the upholstery of the chair and simply stared at his back bent slightly over the keys. I was so wrapped up in my own fury and sorrow that I didn't even hear what he was playing.

After a couple of tunes, he got up from the piano and stood before me. He seemed to have lost his confident manner altogether. Like a small boy begging, he stood facing my chair—too far away for me to touch him—and begged, "Will you take care of me? Will you take me home?"

I studied him. He looked young, fragile and wasted. Lost—not dislocation but perdition.

My heart felt as though it were on hold. I could end this by a single gesture of head or hand. I, myself, could disappear into the black, cold wildness of the night and leave this pathetic creature to a fate he perhaps deserved, though I hadn't allowed myself to picture what that fate must inevitably be.

"No, Matthew," I said, "I will not take you home if you have drugs. I'll get thrown out."

"Okay," he said, "okay …" with the eagerness to please of a puppy, "I'll flush the drugs …"

He disappeared through a second door at the side of the room. Again it occurred to me that I might rise and walk out and leave him here. Again I did not. He came back shortly and grinned and said, "There, they're gone."

I had no idea what he'd really done with the drugs. I sat immobile in the chair watching him jitter his need for my acceptance in nervous little dancing gestures, waiting for me to say, "There's a good boy." The sight of him should have repelled me totally.

"I'll play more for you," he said, moving toward the piano. "Come and sit beside me."

I did. He began to play and sing, his voice gruff and pained, and, despite its rustiness, clearly professional.

I listened and as I listened, something in me started to break. I couldn't stand it anymore. I looked sideways at him, maybe I put my hand on his to make him stop the music. "Matthew," I said, "Who are you? Where did you come from?"

He stared at me. Fear danced in the deep eyes, a small white figure gyrating in the distant blackness. "I am who I said I was and I am from where I said I was from."

CHAPTER THIRTEEN

I KEPT MY EYES on him.

"I don't care about your wonderful house or your marvellous career or your important contacts," I told him. "All I care about is the wonderful person I've seen inside you. If you have some terrible problem, it's all right. I'll care about you anyway."

He smiled. "That's very sweet," he said, "but …"

And then I told him about the song. About the fact that it was credited to someone else. He jumped to his own defence immediately. He said he'd allowed the other person to take credit because he'd been so young himself at the time. He said—just as my brother had said—that the songbooks were often wrong. And then he began to play several famous songs that had been recorded by well-known singers but written by lesser-known composers—to prove that such mistakes were often made.

Then he sang me two songs I'd never heard—lovely songs that he said were also his. He told me that if I wanted a list of people to call about him, he'd be happy to supply names and numbers—but then the mystery would be gone. "You, too," he said to me, "are full of mystery." He played a little longer, then told me more about his wonderful house—"our" house. He tried to teach me to sing one of the pretty songs he'd written. Then he asked me once again to take him home.

Back out in the night, the weather was wilder than ever, but a frenetic joy seemed to have overtaken Matthew as we hailed a cab. Despite the now bitter cold, he wrapped me in his coat—leaving him in only the panther sweater. He kept saying, "I'll get sick and you'll have to take care of me …."

In the cab, he couldn't seem to stop kissing me nor to restrain himself from declaring, "You are the love of my life."

We decided we were starved and we headed for the Terminal, but first I had a package I had to drop off at the place where I did volunteer work. It was, by now, 11 p.m., and I felt reckless and young and important. It was the first time in my life I'd ever taken a taxi to one place and asked it to wait while I completed an errand before going on to another place. I left my purse in the back seat of the cab as I ran to the door, through freezing rain, to deliver my parcel. I heard Matthew give instructions to the cab driver as though he often took cabs from one place to several others. He said he'd wait for me in the back.

When we got to the Terminal, he told me he'd spent all his money on the drugs, so I paid for the cab.

The streets were slick with frozen rain. Holding onto each other for dear life, we slid our way from the cab to the door of the Terminal, and giggling, burst in out of the hostile night. Matthew threw off his coat and insisted that he had to sit in the booth on the same side of the table as me, so that we touched all along one side as I ate.

He seemed enormously happy and was full of talk about our future. He loved to talk about how he would go out on the road and I would be waiting for him in our house. He expressed fear that I might be lonely there. I asked him whether any of the band members' women travelled with them. Matthew froze for an instant, then turned to me and said, "I don't think you would want that. I don't think you would want to see how all those eighteen-year-olds are always throwing themselves at me."

I bought this. I bought everything he said all evening. I also bought the fries, the hamburger, all the beers, and a cab to take us back to my place through the glaring, frozen streets.

The next morning, the whole world was covered with a thick blanket of soft white snow. And Matthew had begun to ask me to promise him that I would never leave him. "Promise me. Promise."

And I did.

Without his asking, I gave him twenty dollars, because I knew he had no cash. He said "dollars" the way only a person from Boston could pronounce that word. I paid attention. I was soon to hear him mention dollars again.

Together we walked through the drifted snow to get to the subway. It was ruining Matthew's expensive leather shoes, but he seemed not to care at all. I found this odd in so fastidious a man.

As had become our routine, he got off at Yonge and Bloor and I went to work, already looking forward to his calling me at 7:30 as he had promised. All afternoon, I could smell him on me. It made me half afraid and half proud. I cancelled a course I was supposed to teach and a public appearance I was supposed to make. I decided when and how I would quit my job. I didn't think about the fact that I had known Matthew for fewer than nine days.

At 7:30 on the dot, he called. There was a lot of noise in the background. It was, he said, a party because it was the last day of the video. He was excited, too, because he was working on a deal to get himself three weeks' worth of additional work in town so that he could stay with me until I could finish the book I was working on—which was nearly done—and make arrangements to go back with him. So we would never have to be apart again before we were married.

I had expected him to say that he'd be late at the party. I had even half-hoped he might have invited me along. Instead, he said he'd meet me at the Terminal in an hour and a half.

When he arrived, he was extremely agitated and said he was very drunk—though he seemed the same as always to me. He sat opposite me in the booth. He seemed to vibrate with nervousness. He ordered drinks and he began to talk. He said I acted as though I wouldn't be coming home with him. He said in the morning he'd listened to me as I talked to people on the phone and it sounded as though I planned to spend my future alone.

I had no answer to this, except to shake my head, to reach across the table and take his hands between mine. I could feel him begin to calm down.

After a while, be became quite relaxed. He drank. He smiled and said, "You never asked me why I wear the same clothes all the time …"

No. I never did. Did I?

I kept silent, and he went on. "It's because of continuity," he said, assuming I knew the technical term, which I did. "Now that the video is over, I can wear anything I want."

We discussed this for a while, kicking around the fact that Matthew had not really worn the same clothes each day because he'd borrowed shirts from me and one day hadn't even worn the panther sweater at all. We both knew there had to be a lie in this somewhere, but neither could face it. I believed with half my heart that he was lying and with the other half that he was not.

I had gotten to the Terminal a little early and was reading *Cosmopolitan* before he arrived. Matthew knew more about fashion and designers and fine china and international cuisine than anyone I had ever met. He also had exquisite manners at all times. This made discussing things with him a sophisticated and cultured pleasure. We began to discuss the woman on the cover of the magazine, and as he so often was, Matthew was brilliant.

He pointed out that a cover photograph is but a frozen instant—a carefully orchestrated moment. He said that offstage from such a shot was a whole brigade of people ready to rush in and correct the slightest imperfection.

In contrast, he said, beauty in real life was unfrozen. It had staying power. It was real. He said he had dated many very beautiful women in his time and told the story of one woman he had slept with who had been on the cover of *Vogue*. He said she had made him promise that he wouldn't look at her without her makeup, which she took off and put on out of sight of Matthew—insisting on staying in the pitch dark at all other times.

The upshot of all this was that I was a true beauty, much more desirable than the frozen beauty in the picture.

We finished our drinks and went home and spent our hours together in bed. Matthew asked me to promise yet again that I would never leave him, and I promised. I went to sleep smiling and I woke up smiling, too.

CHAPTER FOURTEEN

THAT MORNING, WE SAT in bed and calmly discussed the plans for our future. Matthew would keep trying to sign a deal for the next three weeks. I would finish writing my book, and then, together, we would go home to his house. We would marry. I would establish myself as his wife and wait for him while he travelled until he decided that it was time to stop. I would be faithful—unlike, he implied, his first wife.

He would call the two gay artists who regularly house-sat for him and tell them he was coming home—but not alone this time.

He would provide for me. I would not have to work—and therefore would not have to worry about immigration. He himself, he said, had—of course—a green card, since he had never relinquished his Canadian citizenship.

We spoke of these things very calmly, very reasonably. After, we had a coffee and talked some more.

Then Matthew asked me for three hundred and fifty dollars.

I was stunned. My heart dropped. The night before, he had repaid me the twenty he'd borrowed, and as he'd handed me the money, I had thought, "This is a set-up. This is to make me think that he can borrow more and more, and I'll believe he'll repay me."

And now, it seemed, my instinct had been right.

But how could I refuse to give him the money? He knew I had money because he'd seen me cash cheques. We had just discussed our marriage. How could I say no? Especially when he swore it was just a loan for a few days and that he'd transfer funds from the States right away to provide for the fact that he was staying three weeks longer than he'd expected.

With forced cheerfulness, I told him I'd give him a cheque. "No—" he said, "it would be too hard to cash."

"Of course," I said, offering to take him to my bank and cash it for him.

As we left the house to go to the bank, I tried to remind myself that what Matthew said about transferring funds made sense.

On the way to the bank, Matthew was shaking. He spoke wildly about flying down to Florida for a single day for me to meet his parents.

When we got to the bank—a different one from the other I'd been to—he refused to come into the building. Instead, he offered to go across the street to wait for me at McDonald's—where I had told him I was planning to have a coffee. He said he'd never been in McDonald's before.

I cashed two cheques and got a thick wad of cash—like the ones he'd been flashing the previous week—and crossed the street and found him smiling at me near the counter of McDonald's. He'd got me food and found us a table. I handed him the wad. He was still dreadfully nervous. And so was I.

But he kept talking about our wedding—which country would I prefer to hold it in? Who would stand up for us? He made it sound like the most logical choice for him would be to have Neil Young be his best man, but he said he didn't want that sort of publicity.

I listened to him in fearful silence.

He talked about introducing me properly to his community, about putting a notice in the Hartford paper. He smiled across at me and said, "Why, you've never seen me in my good suits, have you?"

I felt as I listened to this that I was slipping farther and farther away from all that was familiar—from reality as I had always known it—into some new kind of reality that left me without footing and without breath, like a stranger in a new country with slippery soil and a vastly different altitude from her own.

As always, we took the subway and Matthew got off at Yonge and Bloor and I went to work. And if I wondered why he was taking the same route as before, when the video was now finished, I didn't make myself answer. Somehow I already knew for sure that when I saw him again, he would not be wearing one of his good suits.

That night he called me at 6:30 because we had agreed that—for the first time—we were to eat supper at my place. He would have come at once, he said, but I told him my landlady was down in my apartment doing her laundry and Matthew thought it better to stay away for an hour or so. I made a large salad and heated some soup and put out cheese and croissants and wine, and everything was ready when he arrived.

As happened now every night, he was extremely nervous when he showed up. He said he'd just come from meeting with the African he'd mentioned in our very first conversation, the man to whom he had promised that he would go to Africa. Now, he said, he'd just told the man that he'd fallen in love and decided he couldn't go to Africa after all. Matthew said he was feeling terribly upset about this. With burning intensity, his black eyes searched my face. "Will you think less of me for not going?" he asked.

"Of course not," I answered—since I'd thought the whole thing foolish from the start, anyway.

Matthew smiled, breathed out a sigh of relief. "That's what I was worried about most," he said as he took off his coat and we sat down to supper after turning off most of the lights, since Matthew said he had "a thing about light."

"I gave that African a thousand dollars," Matthew said.

The first thing that popped into my mind was to question Matthew as to how he could possibly have accomplished this. I had never seen him with a chequebook and his "funds" were not supposed to arrive for another five days.

The second thing that popped into my mind was to question whether Matthew had paid the man in American or Canadian funds. If his story about living in the States was true, surely this would have come up.

We began to eat, Matthew, as always, taking almost nothing. The only thing he seemed to like was the pure olive oil I'd bought for the salad. "That is a very fine oil," he said a couple of times.

He spoke some more of his decision not to go to Africa. In the middle of this discussion, he stopped, looked across the darkened table at me, and laughing said, "I felt like such a fool when he took the cheque and said to me, 'Is this American or Canadian money?'"

I was beginning to be so confused, I no longer knew what to think. Many of the things I'd worried about before, Matthew had excuses for and had offered them before I'd even mentioned what I was thinking about.

He said, for instance, that he'd ordered a pizza and had had to find my address. That explained the left-out tax form.

Also, one day, I took a drink from the mug I'd found with the lipstick mark and discovered I'd just made an identical mark. Clearly, the first mark had been mine, too.

And he had long since given me back the keys to my place.

As we ate, Matthew said it looked very good for the jingles he was trying to get that three-week commission to write. He'd met with a Mr. Santo, he said, a man who was quite impressed with Matthew. It seemed as though the extra work would soon be a sure thing.

Thus far, Matthew had still never changed his clothes, never showed any ID or keys, never had any possessions on him, never mentioned friends and always dropped names as though he were a spring cloud dropping rain.

After eating supper—which was only, for him, a bit of salad and a taste of soup—he wanted to go to bed, though it was barely eight p.m. Though I would have preferred to actually do something with him, something other than just being together, I acquiesced to his insistence.

Our warmth and closeness, our passion, our laughter and our discussions continued unabated—intensified in every way, in fact. We—or mostly Matthew—talked about our future, our house. He said over and over that he wished he were capable of having children—he seemed obsessed by this theme.

He asked me to promise yet again that I wouldn't leave him. He told me about his ex-wife—the only woman he talked about seriously. He said she was a university professor, specializing in quantum physics, from a wealthy Canadian family and that they had been divorced ten years before.

He said again how surprised he was to be so very in love—that he couldn't believe how in love he was. He begged me to hold him in my arms, to hug him as hard as I could. When I did, he asked me to hug even harder than that.

In the middle of the night, either before we slept, or after awaking out of sleep and loving, I lay atop him, his slender body nearly completely covered by mine. In the depth of the night, I felt the strange power of our union. "Matthew," I whispered into the total blackness of the room, "I don't know whether our plans will work out, but whatever happens, I think we are already bound together now."

"I know."

CHAPTER FIFTEEN

More and more Matthew began to lose his air of confidence and strength. He began to say to me, "I am very fragile." I was puzzled by this, though I knew it was true. I'd not yet realized, though, what it might mean.

Somehow, after our little supper, we managed to spend fourteen hours in bed. It occurred to me that Matthew and I had actually done almost nothing together except sit at the Terminal and lie in bed, but that thought was pushed to the back of my mind along with certain others.

Like the fact that he never seemed to read anything—no books, no newspapers, no magazines, no menus. Though he occasionally talked about movies, he didn't seem to know a thing about recent ones, as though he hadn't seen one in years.

That morning, we got up, had coffee, talked—our usual routine. We took the subway together. He said he'd call me later, and he did.

I was waiting for him rather late that night at the Terminal. He arrived and Cynthia set down his brand of beer without his asking. He smiled. He seemed, more than ever before, perfectly calm. He was obviously, though, very happy about something. He seemed different and it took me a minute to realize what the difference was. It was that he seemed normal.

He insisted on sitting beside me in the booth rather than opposite, and he revealed that he'd been totally successful in his dealings with reference to the jingles. He said he'd closed a deal: one sixty-second spot and two thirty-second spots. He was going to get a one-time payment of eighteen thousand dollars for this work.

He said he was thrilled to have accomplished this, and that the biggest thrill was to be able to share his good fortune with me. Not only was he happy, he was hungry.

He ordered, and ate, a large plate of French fries. And then he ordered another.

It was the happiest time we'd had yet—which was saying something. He told me he wanted to buy me something—not too extravagant. He always maintained that he hated extravagance, that it was inelegant. So he wanted to spend, he said, only about four thousand dollars.

He told me he'd take me to New York to buy a dress and he spoke of several designers, some of whose names I recognized and some not.

I said maybe jewellery would be nice. He didn't like this idea because he thought four thousand was too small a sum to spend for a good piece of jewellery, but he said he knew a goldsmith, so …

Then I thought of something I'd wanted all my life. I asked him if his house was big enough for a grandfather clock.

"Our house," he corrected. "And yes. Yes, of course it is. If that's what you want, that's what I'll buy you. When we get home I'll buy you a grandfather clock."

We were both in a wonderful mood that night. How we joked and laughed and touched! How he drew for me a verbal picture of his friends, the two gay painters who were house-sitting for him—and of another of his friends, a sports car dealer. "You'll meet them," he said with evident joy, "you'll meet them all."

On and on we went, so joyous in our pretense, so together, so happy, and so beautiful that the shabby bar seemed to glow with radiance, and even the half-gone old drunks sat up straighter against the patched red vinyl of the booths and grinned more widely in their reeling, toothless way.

As we left—Matthew paying as always—he turned to me, stopping me in my tracks. "I was so lonely before I met you," he said, "now, to be without you would …"

The pause was too pregnant, too slick. It sickened me a little. I asked him why he would worry about being without me after the elaborate plans we'd discussed for staying together for as long as possible. But he didn't answer. He just turned away and we resumed our walk.

All the snow was gone now and it had begun to rain. Side by side, very close, we walked back to my place, talked, went to bed. Everything was dreamlike and wonderful.

In the morning, Friday, a few minutes before we left, when I was once again unprepared, hurried and too stunned to refuse, Matthew asked me for another three hundred dollars.

Now, I was terrified. I could only agree. Just before asking, he had called the airport and asked the price of a ticket to Boston on the pretense of wanting to know because of our plans to fly there in three weeks.

I was so confused, so disappointed, so scared I could not speak to him as we rushed to the bank, hurrying so I wouldn't be late for work. Again, he refused to come anywhere near the building, but loitered on an opposite corner, then slunk across the street when I came out with the cash clutched in my trembling hand as if I'd robbed instead of being robbed.

I handed him the wad. I felt a total fool, but I knew I dared not risk refusing him now for fear of what strange or ugly thing might happen if I did.

He tried to make conversation, but I just couldn't talk. A thousand thoughts spiralled in my brain while he babbled on about some man he'd met who did aerial photography. He said maybe the man would take us up in his plane. He reached into the pocket of his raincoat, which I now noticed was spotted in front, and pulled out a worn business card that had printed on it the name of some private flying outfit.

This attempt to capture my attention was totally pathetic. It was the tactic of a vagrant, of a desperate street person. I'd seen it before. Some sorry individual pulls out a letter or a photograph, grappling, by means of a grubby piece of paper, for some lost respectability, some connection with the person from whom he is begging. I could not respond at all. Even pity failed me.

We got on the subway, and, as always, Matthew sat close to me. We did not speak during the whole trip. No discussion of videos or Beethoven or sports cars or art.

When he got off at Yonge and Bloor, I got off with him. This, of course, was not our usual way, but I pretended I was upset over the prospect of quitting my job, which we had discussed and which I'd said I would do that day in order to have more time to get ready for our plans.

In fact, I got off because I wanted to kiss Matthew goodbye, to hold him one more time. I was one hundred per cent certain that I would never see him again. He had almost seven hundred dollars of my money—enough to get to Boston and from there to Hartford with no trouble. He didn't need me for anything more.

And when we parted and he failed to say—for the only time—"I'll call you," I was sure it was over.

I got on the train. As it pulled away, Matthew waved at me. "Goodbye forever," I thought. "Goodbye."

I was so certain he was gone for good.

Yet one infinitesimal part of me whispered in a voice I could not hear, only feel the vibration of deep inside. "It's not going to be as easy as that …"

CHAPTER SIXTEEN

When I got to work I tried frantically to get a free minute to phone Ruth, and after an hour or two, I finally managed it.

When I told her about the money, she said I was hopeless and that she was ready to give up on me. Despite my distress at what she said, I didn't blame her. I felt the same way. She told me to calm down, and that after work she'd do what she could to help me out.

Somehow I got through the afternoon.

I got home and waited, sure Matthew would not call. Ruth, however, did call, and she said I should wait only a little longer, then should go out with her. She was quite certain Matthew must have left town.

I asked her to call information in Hartford to ask if there was a number listed for Matthew, figuring that even if it was unlisted, they'd tell us whether his name was in the directory.

I waited some more.

In a little while, the phone rang. It was Ruth. There was no one by Matthew's name listed in Hartford—or anywhere in the surrounding areas, either.

I decided to call the manager of the Highlander—the one who'd been so excited about Matthew—to ask him what he knew. But he was off that night. All I could do was leave a number for him to get back to me.

Then I decided to call the police. They listened patiently to my story and told me I could have an officer come to the house and report a "suspicious person." I just wasn't ready to do that to Matthew, whoever or whatever he was.

It got to be 8:30. Everything led to the inescapable conclusion that Matthew was gone: the money, the call to the airline he'd made that morning, the fact that he—for the only time—hadn't said he'd phone when he'd left me at the subway, the fact that indeed he hadn't called.

I changed my clothes and went out with Ruth.

We had dinner, and during it I felt calm, relieved somehow. Ruth kept saying I was taking "it" well. It seemed to me I wasn't taking "it" at all.

After dinner, we visited friends of Ruth's—lively, interesting people I'd been with and enjoyed several times before. I enjoyed them now, but I began to feel extremely tired. I also began to feel the presence of Matthew lurking somewhere, lying in wait.

Among my friend's friends, I got such an overwhelming feeling of the joys of normalcy that all I had experienced with Matthew seemed appalling and repellent in comparison. As I sat among these pleasant, ordinary people, laughing and talking, I felt a sense of longing—profound longing for the life I, too, had had less than two weeks before. I felt I had lost my life. I wanted it back.

But then I thought of the strange promises of my demon lover, thought of him beneath me in the black night swearing that we were one. I felt lost, adrift between two worlds.

When I got home, he was waiting for me, crouched in the rain, peering into my window like a mad man, swearing he could see me sleeping down in the apartment, even though I was standing beside him. He was delirious—drunk, stoned, crazy, or all three. Absurdly, he clutched in his hand a bright, crisp, new Blue Jays baseball cap.

I had a hard time convincing him that I was beside him and that there was no one beyond the window into which he kept looking. "But the light's on down there," he kept saying. "The light's on ... And the bed's all messed up. Somebody's there. Somebody's in that bed ..."

I tried to soothe him, to draw him away from the window, to coax him in out of the rain. "I left the light on, myself," I told him, "because I didn't want to come home to a dark place. And I'm the one who messed up the bed. I was taking a nap."

He was utterly terrified, crying and shaking and insisting he had to know who it was who was down there.

"Nobody, Matthew, nobody is down there. I'm up here ..."

He started to ask me where I'd been, as if it were inconceivable that I hadn't waited for him to call whenever he'd been ready to call.

"Come on," I said, "let's get out of the rain. Let's get inside."

"I feel so bad," he cried, "so bad. And Monday I have to start that work. I should go home. I should just go home."

His reference to the jingles he'd said he'd contracted to write struck me. It struck me as sounding oddly true, as if he had in fact somehow gotten that work and was now, though fairly incoherent, remembering that he'd set himself up for a major obligation. Scared as I was myself, it struck me that if he'd made that up, if he were pretending, his mention of this now made him the most acute, sensitive, clever actor I'd ever known. Either some of the things he said were for real or else he was so consummate a performer, so keen an observer of life, that his act commanded a respect that his life never could.

I managed to calm him down only a very little, but it was enough to get him inside out of the wind and the rain.

He kept asking me where I'd been, and I kept telling him. He was shaking, but he soon took off his clothes. He would not let me touch him and kept making a strange motion with his hands and wrists, fending me off not by striking out at me but by bending his hands inward toward his chest.

He said he was terrified of me—that he didn't know who or what I was …

I pulled out the bed, helped him out of his wet clothes, and we sat side by side on the edge of the mattress. He became calmer. He'd been waiting for me, he said, for three hours at the Terminal.

I didn't even try to explain that I'd had no way of knowing he'd be there, though I did tell him I thought he was about to disappear when he'd left me at the subway that day.

"But I didn't disappear," he said. "I'm here …"

We lay down and he became calmer still. He no longer seemed drunk or stoned. He did not smell of alcohol. In fact, he never did smell of alcohol—ever.

I told him I'd phoned Hartford and that there was nobody living there or near there who had his name.

"That's easy," he said, "the phone is listed under my brother's name."

I persisted. "How did you give that guy a cheque for Africa? You don't have a chequebook."

"Yeah," he said, "yeah, I have a chequebook."

"But you don't have any ID. How can you travel from here to Hartford and back with no ID? I cross the border myself all the time. You have to have ID."

"No," Matthew said cryptically, "it can be done without."

I asked him question after question, and though some of his replies were very odd and made nearly no sense, he valiantly strove to come up with an excuse for every single accusation.

By now I was well aware how pathetic he was. I had long feared he was dangerous. Yet in his presence, I felt far more pity for him than fear.

He knew I had to know almost certainly that he was lying, but he knew, too, that his lies still had power over me.

I told him I couldn't stand it anymore, that unless I met the people he was supposedly staying with—though, of course, he'd still not got different clothes—unless I was actually introduced to someone who knew him, I had to assume that what he had been telling me about himself was untrue.

His immediate answer was that he didn't like the apartment where he was supposed to be staying because the neighbourhood was too full of gay men!

CHAPTER SEVENTEEN

It occurred to me, as it had before, though without my making much of it, that Matthew talked about gay men an awful lot for a man who was straight himself. There were the gay artists who were supposedly in "his" house. There were the gays in the neighbourhood of his "friends." There was his strange comment the first night we met, a comment that came back to me later. He'd said he often spent time among handsome men.

What could all this mean?

Yet, as always seemed to happen, something distracted me from questioning him. What distracted me now was that he rolled over on his stomach as if weeping into the pillow and cried, "I should just leave. I should just go home."

"Where, Matthew?" I asked him. "Where would you go?"

"Hartford," was all he said.

And of course, he did not go home, he did not leave. He seemed to be crying. I lay on top of him, full of sorrow for him, knowing full well that most certainly I would soon be full of sorrow for myself.

He mumbled that he had made up his mind that he must go to Africa after all. He was sorry, he said, but that was the only answer. As he fell into the death-like stupor that, for him, passed as sleep, he quite clearly said, "Don't worry, I've spoken to my lawyer. You're taken care of. Everything I have is in your name."

I fell in a deep sleep at once, and we didn't wake until late the next day, even though our sleep was interrupted by a knock on the door by the landlady, who needed to come down for something to do with the furnace. I told her I wasn't up yet, and we slept for hours more.

At noon, it was obvious that she wouldn't be put off, so we got up and Matthew insisted on hiding in the washroom when the landlady's boyfriend came down to check out some fuses.

A little while later, Matthew dressed and prepared to leave. I asked him what he would do that day, a little surprised that we'd not be doing something together, which seemed the natural thing for two people who'd sworn they couldn't bear to be apart until their "marriage."

He said he was going to do some errands, then arrange for me to meet the friends I'd insisted on meeting. There had been no mention recently of the fact that Matthew, nearly two weeks after I'd met him, had never changed his clothes except to borrow my shirts and socks, though a day or two before, he'd said that he didn't want to go to his friends' place "just to change."

As he prepared to go, there was still the tiniest shred of belief in me, but mostly I was biding my time, trying to think of a way to force him to tell me the truth about himself. Somehow I thought the truth would bring about the result I now saw as absolutely necessary: to get him away from me, away from my place, out of my life.

He promised to call at 3:30 p.m. It was now 1:30, his usual time for leaving me. Off he went.

Despite all that was going on, I calmly sat down and wrote the last chapter of my novel.

But 3:30 came and went and there was no word from Matthew.

I did, however, talk to the manager of the Highlander. I noticed, as before, what an exceptionally jumpy man he was. He was quite friendly, but I was no longer sure I should mention Matthew—and I didn't, asking him a few questions about one of the topics we'd discussed the night we'd met. He seemed quite satisfied with that.

I also erased the tape on my answering machine from the night before. That morning, before Matthew had left, I had played it back. It was full of frantic, desperate calls from Matthew, his voice panic-stricken, swearing I was there but not picking up the phone, begging to know where I was and why I wasn't answering. "Where are you?" he begged to know over and over again. "I can't believe you're not there. I can't. I can't …"

Anyone, it seemed to me, anyone with the least shred of dignity would have cringed with embarrassment at hearing such a display played back. The desperation was so blatant, so passionate as to be almost subhuman. Matthew listened to that tape and laughed.

Another thing I did in his absence that Saturday was to examine a small vial of pills he'd brought home the night before. He said he'd been to an herbalist and told the man about his long and fruitless battle to regain his fertility. The herbalist, he'd said, had told him that if he took these pills, he'd be fertile within the year.

I could tell nothing by examining the pills themselves, the little bottle they came in, nor the round dot of a label on the top with numbers and letters written in pencil.

But I recalled that, before he'd left that Saturday morning, Matthew had told me he now felt foolish that he had believed what the herbalist had said.

It got to be five o'clock and—fearing another panic attack—I erased the usual message on my answering machine and constructed and recorded one that would reassure Matthew if he called and found me gone. I had to grocery shop, and soon the stores would be closed.

I went first to the bank where just the day before, I'd withdrawn the second lot of money for him. I felt almost ashamed to go in, as if they would wonder what sort of a fool I was to come into the bank so often.

Weatherwise, it was a horrid evening—full yet again of wild rain and unrelenting wind. I went to a neighbourhood grocer and bought far more food than I needed for myself, though I don't know who I thought would eat it.

When I got home at six, he'd still not called. Finally, though, at six-thirty, he did.

He said he was at a friend's house and that the friend had invited us to dinner, that the friend just happened to live right in my neighbourhood and that he and the friend would come over to pick me up within the half hour.

Though in my heart I knew that this, too, was a ruse, as always, I was happy to have finally heard from Matthew and happy at the prospect of soon being with him again. I had got to the point where I was almost praying that I'd never see him again, and yet, my first thought on seeing him was, "Thank God, you're back."

He arrived very soon after the phone call, and he had the look on his face that by now I realized meant he was up to something. He was nervous, too, but it was an excited kind of nervousness—that of a kid who has lucked out and is sure he's going to get away with something just because he was fortuitously snatched from the jaws of doom by the fate that is kind to the bad.

He asked me if I would bring along a copy of one of my books to autograph for the wife of his friend. I was happy to lend him this credibility, even though I knew the evening he was now offering as his own credibility was as suspect as everything else about him.

CHAPTER EIGHTEEN

My suspicions were confirmed before we even got to our host's home.

I walked out to the curb in front of my place and there I saw a brand new van. So far so good. Inside the van was a man I trusted the moment I set eyes on him. He was warm, obviously intelligent, very kind-looking. He even turned out to be an exceptionally careful driver.

With Matthew—smirking—sitting on a milk crate between the driver's and passenger's seat, where I sat, we took off for the friend's—Bob's—nearby home.

But first, Matthew insisted, we had to stop off at the neighbourhood beer store for a 12-pack—which he also insisted on paying for. He got out of the van and headed into the store.

Which left Bob and me alone. I turned to him and said, "And how long have you known Matthew?"

"Well," the kindly Bob answered in his sweet voice, "that's a funny thing. I met Matthew playing in a small club downtown about three years ago. I hadn't seen him since, but this afternoon I was in a bar near here and I saw him and I said to myself—hey, I know him! So I went up and struck up a conversation. He remembered me and was really happy to see me. Some coincidence, eh?"

Yeah. Some coincidence.

But there was no way I was going to blow Matthew's evening, because Bob and his wife Sue were absolutely lovely people. They welcomed me into their home. For a good long time, Bob entertained us by playing his guitar and singing. One of his own songs was so wonderful that Matthew and I both insisted on hearing it again. Matthew sang a bit, too. How I loved to hear him—even when I knew his wrecked, pained, painful voice was the voice of deceit and despair no matter what he'd made Bob and Sue believe about himself. How some things will scream the truth when everything else about a person is a lie.

I could tell by the unmistakable deference with which Bob treated Matthew—and by a few of Bob's comments—that Matthew had told him the same story about Neil Young as he'd told me and that Bob had bought it totally, too. I found this sad and confusing, but I forced myself not to weaken. I knew Matthew was a liar. I just wanted to give him a few more happy hours.

And he was happy that night. Our conversation ranged over all sorts of topics. Bob and Sue were very *au courant*, very intelligent, very individual and very sensitive. So were Matthew and I. Never had I so enjoyed an evening of two-couple conversation.

After a little while, Sue asked us if we were hungry. Matthew, who had, of course, never eaten a meal in my presence, said yes.

Sue, as it turned out, had been simmering a pot of quite wonderful shrimp soup, which she now served us with fresh bread and cheddar cheese. As she set the table, I saw Matthew looking at her china. It was truly elegant—simply a white embossed design of a single swirl forming the edge of the plate, then moving inward to change from structure to ornament in a sweep.

Matthew seemed to observe it with resigned longing. He complimented them on their taste in having chosen it. I could tell he was genuinely moved by some emotion that was strong but strongly hidden. I couldn't tell whether it was regret for something he had lost or sorrow over the unattainability of something he would never have. Or both.

Matthew slowly, almost painfully, it seemed to me, ate two whole bowls of soup. He seemed to have to force it down, though he complimented Sue on how exquisite it was.

After the meal, Bob made espresso, and when he took out the machine for it, Matthew leaned toward me and whispered, "We have one of those ..."

"No," I wanted to say. "No, my poor confused love, we do not."

Instead, I merely nodded.

We talked more. Bob mentioned in passing that Matthew was supposed to have given him his address in Hartford, but had forgotten.

"Oh, yes," Matthew said, "I meant to do that. I'll have to write it down."

Fat chance.

At another point in the conversation, I mentioned that I had called the manager of the Highlander. Matthew—who had told me he'd played there the Saturday night I'd been in Utica—reached into his pocket and pulled out a business card from the manager. On the back was written, "Thanks for all the fun." It looked to me very like the same scrawly handwriting on the "autographed" Neil Young record.

When it got to be eleven, we left. The last thing Bob said to Matthew was, "It was fun seeing you again. It's lucky that you missed your plane ..."

"Missed your plane?" I asked as we walked into the rainy night. "What does that mean?"

"Oh," Matthew said, pulling me close against his side, "he just meant that I didn't go straight back to Hartford after the video was done."

We started to walk back the short distance to my place. The night was still windy and rainy and not very warm. I wanted to get home as fast as I could, but Matthew dawdled. We decided to go to the Terminal, decided we were still hungry.

But when we got to the Terminal, it was closing. Another waitress, not Cynthia, was there and she let us know there was no use in coming in.

So we walked down the street a little to another restaurant, a glorified doughnut shop. We ordered gravy and chips—as usual. As he picked at the food on the boring, thick, cheap restaurant plate, Matthew told me again about his own china and the cabinet in which he stored it. He was worried, he said, because the style of the cabinet didn't match the mood or the style of the dishes.

"But when you come," he said, staring at me, "you can change whatever you want ...."

We left and on the way home, I discovered I'd lost an earring. I was content to forget about it, but Matthew insisted on helping me look for it. We retraced our steps for what seemed many long blocks. It was beginning to get quite cold and it still poured rain. We had no umbrella—and the wind would have caught it if we had.

But Matthew seemed to want to stay out as long as possible. No matter what I said, I couldn't get him to hurry home the way I wished we would.

We gave up on the earring. "Thank God," I thought, "Now at least we can head home."

But Matthew was out of cigarettes, which necessitated more tramping along the rain-soaked midnight Danforth.

By the time we got home, I was frozen and drenched. But I didn't complain. For Matthew, it had been a perfect evening. He had had the warmth, acceptance and respect that comes not only from being taken seriously—which, of course, he did not mention—but also the proud knowledge of sharing this acceptance with a woman he felt privileged to be with—which he did mention.

I thought it might be the first and last such evening that poor, lost Matthew would have in a good long time.

CHAPTER NINETEEN

THE NEXT DAY, THOUGH Sunday, was like every other day. We loved, we had coffee, we talked, and Matthew disappeared at one in the afternoon.

He said nothing about where he was going, whether he was coming back or when.

I felt sick all day and wasn't sorry to have the long day at home alone, but when it got to be nine-thirty and I had had no word from him at all, I called Ruth and told her I felt as though I was going out of my mind with fear, disgust, confusion, despair.

I told her I wanted to go to the police.

It was a wild, raging night. Nonetheless, my faithful, dauntless girlfriend came, and together in her car we threaded our way through the dark streets in search of the closest police station, which we eventually found.

It took the duty cop long enough to run Matthew's name and DOB through CPIC for me to figure he had to have something on him, especially when he started writing things down, then turned to me and said, "Do you have an address for this guy?"

"Yeah, sure," I felt like saying. "Mine!" Instead, I just shook my head.

But in the end, all the cop would say was, "I have no reason to tell you he's dangerous. If I were you, though, and he comes by again, I would lock my door and dial 911."

"Not much help," Ruth commented as we left the station.

"No," I answered, "but at least it doesn't sound as though he's a crazed killer or anything." Neither of us laughed.

When we got back to my place, there was a message on my machine.

Matthew had called and said he would call back. Impatience was clear in his taped voice, displeasure at my not being there. I had left a message saying I'd be back at eleven and he said he'd call then. It was now ten-thirty.

Ruth and I wracked our brains to try to figure out what to do next, to think of a way to find out something about Matthew that we could confront him with, presumably to get him to admit to the truth about himself, whatever that was. Somehow we were convinced that if he were forced to tell the truth, he'd also be compelled to leave.

As we sat by the phone, it suddenly occurred to me that there was a possible chain of people that might lead to Dill, the singer, our only mutual acquaintance—the man we'd seen the first day we'd met. Maybe there was someone who knew someone who knew someone who had Dill's unlisted number.

I dialed the first person in the chain.

And soon I had the other number, the one I needed.

It being very late, the recipient of my phone call was not overly happy to hear my voice. It had been a long time since

I'd talked to him, and at first, he seemed reluctant to talk about Matthew, though he recognized the name immediately.

After a little prodding, he began to talk. He painted a picture of Matthew as a pathetic person who told a tall tale—even on stage—and had been considered an object of ridicule for some time. The place Dill mentioned having heard Matthew make a fool of himself often at was a coffeehouse that had had its heyday at least a decade before. Dill told me a joke people used to tell about Matthew's claim that he had once opened for Neil Young. "Opened what?" people said, "Pop bottles?"

He said Matthew was not dangerous, just a sad fool. "And," Dill said, "I've heard he likes the boys in the band, if you know what I mean …."

He said further that he would admit that Matthew had written some good songs and that he was quite a singer, but on the whole, he was a failure and his wild stories the just object of scorn among his fellow musicians.

It sounded like all this had happened a long time ago—as though Matthew had been telling his tale for more than ten years. It also sounded as though Matthew had been very much a Toronto personality rather than someone from out of town.

The last thing our mutual friend said was that it looked like Matthew stuffed socks in his pants.

I knew we were definitely talking about the same man.

I thanked Dill for his help and hung up.

All during our conversation, there had been a strange clicking sound. Both of us had noticed it and had tried to decide whose phone was doing it. "My phone never does that," Dill asserted. "Neither," I swore, "does mine."

When I turned to Ruth and briefly relayed what I'd been told, my only feeling was pity for Matthew. Dill's narrative had been bitter and dismissive, and maybe he spoke out of some negative emotion of his own, resentment or even envy, but what he had said could not be ignored.

I knew I had to confront Matthew with this information, but I was no longer frightened at the prospect. No crazed killer. And no star, either. He was nothing more than the most pathetic of losers—and I had dealt with pathetic losers before.

Ruth offered to stay and help me out. But I told her I would have to handle things myself.

The phone rang. It was Matthew. He asked me whether I was okay. I said yes, wondering why he should be worried.

He answered that he'd tried to get me and that when he heard the busy signal, he'd made an operator cut in on the line to make sure I was okay.

This astounded me. I had never heard of an operator agreeing to cut in on a conversation. My understanding was that you'd have had to convince an operator that it was a matter of life and death before they'd do such a thing.

Nonetheless, I said nothing to Matthew. He seemed nervous and said he was starving and asked me if he should pick up some sandwiches and bring them over.

I found this extremely strange and asked him whether he'd eaten dinner. Of course, he said no. So I said, "Okay, bring food if you'd like." Then we hung up. Matthew's voice had a quality to it that was so similar to the quality it had had the night he'd met Ruth, that I had the uncanny feeling that he knew exactly what she and I had done this night.

Ruth was reluctant to leave, but I felt sure I could handle him. My only concern was that she would run into him on her way out, since he claimed to be calling from the very next street.

When an hour and a half had passed with no sign of him, I gave up and went to bed—not pulling it out, but leaving the futon folded as I did when I slept alone.

As soon as I closed my eyes in the totally dark room, I heard a soft knock on my door.

I went and opened it.

In burst Matthew all full of happy energy and carrying a large bag from a pizza place. He'd had to go from place to place in a cab before finding something open, then finally he did find something open and here he was and he was starving and I must be starving, too, and God he loved me!

I found this whole routine confusing in the extreme, but he wasn't fooling me right now. Though I had no idea what he was and had been up to, I now, at least, knew he was always up to something.

He looked at the bed and smiled and commented, "Oh, you went to bed—and you're sleeping single again," just as if that was nothing to him.

He was so full of energy and so cheery and so hungry—bustling about, searching for forks to eat the pizza pockets he'd bought and talking about how in love with me he was.

He was making me sick. I told him I'd called Dill and told him Dill had told me that the story about Neil Young was nothing but a joke.

CHAPTER TWENTY

He got the angriest I'd ever seen him.

He swore he'd told me before—which he pretty much had—that Dill was his enemy. He said Dill was a nobody. Over and over he said, "You shouldn't have done this, you never should have done this. Now you're going to lose me."

I wasn't falling for it. "Matthew," I said calmly, "I can't lose you. I've never had you. This is all a story, a fantasy."

He had no answer to that. He said I should have called all the people he'd told me about—and he rattled off a long list of impressive names, names he'd been dropping all along.

Remarkably enough, in the middle of all this, we calmed down and we ate. Matthew was not kidding about being very hungry.

When we finished the food, we resumed our discussion. It should have been angry, but there was only the usual fake kind of anger in Matthew, only a stance, a gesture, the saving of face.

I pointed out to him yet again all the odd unexplainable things about him and about our time together. He offered the same lame excuses, some of which made no sense at all. He insisted, for instance, that he had run out of money because his credit card had run out, and how that meant he'd authorized payment, then torn the card in four and thrown it into four separate trash cans—as he had when his other cards had run out.

I had no idea what he was talking about, but it crossed my mind that perhaps he stole credit cards and somehow used them for cash advances, then destroyed them. I thought of the night I'd left him alone in the back of the cab with my purse. I thought of how he'd stared at that purse the day I'd bought my ticket to Utica. I thought of how he'd been perfectly willing to enter one of my banks but that wild horses couldn't draw him into the other. And I thought of how many times I'd lain beside him in the dark of night, drifting off into sleep, convinced he was sleeping, too, when he might have been faking, might have been waiting for me to sleep so that he could get up …

I thought of how he'd had the keys to my place for a whole weekend. Long enough to have had them copied many times over.

I told him that both Ruth and I had called Hartford and found neither him nor his brother listed. At this information, he rattled off a phone number—with the right area code for Connecticut—and told me to call it.

There was no way I could write it down and I didn't ask him to say it again.

When I pressed him about the friends he'd supposedly been staying with, he again gave me the supposed location—in a neighbourhood that I now knew was largely gay. I had looked up the name he'd given me for those friends and there was no listing in the Toronto phone book.

At last, clearly able to tell no more lies—at least for that night—he lay on his stomach and said, "At least let me stay for one more night."

And of course, it being one in the morning and raining unrelentingly, I was not likely to do otherwise. I still pitied him. I lay on top of him, as full of terror and I was of pity, and began to comfort him. And one thing led to another and soon it was I who was lying underneath and he was telling me how tragic it was that he couldn't have children because he knew that in me he'd found the one woman kind enough to be the mother of his daughters and sons.

And I kept saying, "Matthew, this is a dream and you are a dreamer and nothing about this is real. It has to come to an end."

But what he was saying as he bent over me in the soft light, his lean body pale, his dark curls shining, was beautiful. He was describing, as I'd never heard a man describe before, his dreams of fathering—what he imagined it would feel like to know that he had made me pregnant, that we were one in the child I'd carry in my body.

His words, his kisses, his gentle touches were so tempting, so impossible to resist, that for the first time, I understood why nature had connected sex and parenthood.

My whole body was reaching for him, even though I refused to answer his passionate musings. He sighed my name and swore I was capable of driving a man crazy. Then, he stretched out beside me and fell into the death-like stillness he called sleep, and so did I.

In the morning when I awoke and looked at him he was utterly beautiful—the perfect body, the insouciant curls, the mauve perfection of his largesse. For the only time in my life, I knew what it was to desire a body regardless of the soul that inhabited it—or my own soul. But I knew that sooner or later

I'd be called upon to pay dearly for these strange pleasures to which I had given myself totally.

When we rose to dress, I knew our time was done. Matthew, looking more boyish and fragile than ever, was nearly dressed—all in his own clothes this time, the same clothes, of course, as those he'd been wearing the first day. He was sitting on a chair, and I went over to him and stood before him.

"Matthew," I said, "this thing between us has been great, but I have to get back to my ordinary life."

He looked stricken, but not surprised. In fact, the change in his expression was imperceptible. It was just that suddenly he looked very weak, very vulnerable, very in need of help.

"If I had the wherewithal," I said, "I would keep you with me for the rest of my life, but I can't. It's hard enough taking care of one person …"

As I spoke, I stroked his black curls. He sat perfectly immobile and silent beneath my touch. I sat opposite him and watched the boyish tragic beauty in the planes of his face. I couldn't help thinking that he looked like the kind of man another man would love to love. We said nothing. After a while, he got up and went to the washroom. He was a long, long time in there, and I began to be afraid.

So I got up and went to the door and knocked on it, fearful of what I'd hear.

But he came out. Without speaking, he put on his panther sweater and went over to the dresser where he'd put the ashtray after smoking his very last cigarette. "I'm sorry to have to do this," he said with a little laugh, "but …"

He began to dig through the ashes looking for a butt long enough to light. He didn't find one.

I went over to him and looked up at him, and much as I still feared and pitied him—for he seemed truly and irredeemably desperate now—I respected him, too, because he still carried himself with unmistakable dignity.

"Matthew," I said, staring into his handsome face, "tell me what you were doing the day I met you—before you came to that wake ..."

With downcast eyes and in a voice so low it was almost impossible to hear, he said, "I was wandering ..."

"And where did you sleep the night before you slept with me the first time?"

He nearly whispered the words.

"The baths ..."

CHAPTER TWENTY-ONE

"THEN YOU GO WITH men sometimes?" I asked, sure he must.

"No."

He raised his eyes. His voice seemed choked with tears and his face was stolid, pale, beautiful and very sad. He looked down at me and he said, "I just wish I'd met you when I was better …"

My heart felt as though it had started to bleed.

"Oh Matthew," I said, throwing my arms around his neck, "What are we going to do?"

I must have known quite well even then that we were going to do nothing.

After only a few moments, he stepped out of my embrace and headed for the door. "Can I call you later," he asked, "to find out how you are?"

It seemed a strange question, but I couldn't stop myself from nodding yes.

It was early afternoon. Somehow I passed the hours until it was time for me to go to school. I felt so sad I could hardly lift my eyes. It seemed to me I suddenly understood the grief of widows.

But I sat through the whole class. By luck, the man who sat next to me was one of the police officers in the course and a person who I knew lived not far from me. I decided that, after class, I would ask him for a ride home, and that on the way I would tell him my sad, weird tale.

He listened patiently, despite my many protestations of shame and self-disgust over what I was rapidly coming to feel was an appallingly stupid situation to have got myself into.

But he assured me that many people had had such experiences, that some liars were very skillful and that there was nothing to be ashamed of. On the other hand, he said, some truth-tellers had very strange stories indeed.

When I told him I had asked where Matthew lived and had been told "the baths," he said that meant the Roman Baths in the heart of the gay prostitution district at Wellesley and Bay. The cop said that not everyone who frequented the baths was gay. He said they served as a central storehouse for the downtown drug trade and that there was constant traffic between the baths and the St. Charles gay bar on Yonge Street. He said he knew what he was talking about because he'd busted both places.

When I told him that Matthew seemed to disappear every day between one and nine p.m., he said that, on the one hand, if the man were a musician, those were not odd hours to be working—the cocktail hours. But on the other hand, the early afternoon was when the drug trade traditionally got under way each day.

I told him about the cop the night before, about his running Matthew through CPIC and how long it had seemed to take and how the cop had copied something down and asked if I had an address.

He said it was possible that the computer had listed prior arrests and charges on Matthew for drug offenses.

Then my friend turned to me and said, "Look, if I was a con, I'd know how to work you the minute I laid eyes on you. You're a nice lady—a very nice lady. All I'd have to do would be to make you feel sorry for me and I'd have it made. I'm sure the guy valued everything he got from you. Obviously there was an emotional thing going on—plus he got a bed and an address.

"But," he went on, "this sounds like a guy who might be on his way down. He's done without you for thirty-five years. He can do without you now. When a person tries to lift somebody like that up, at first it's great and both people are lifted. But pretty soon, he's back down and he's dragging you down, too. And then he starts resenting you—because you're successful and he's not.

"There was a case a while back where a young man took up with an elderly woman. He ended up raping her, beating her, and taking just about all she had. And she didn't even want to press charges ….

"Look," he said, "I can tell how drawn you are to the guy, and I can understand it. I've been drawn to losers myself—and got burned, too. But let me tell you a story. I loved somebody once, a wonderful woman, but a woman not my wife. I'm a cop, it's true," he laughed, "but to me, once I'm married, I'm married for life. No matter how tempted I was, I knew what I had to do. I said to this woman, 'I wish I could have it both ways', and she said, 'you can', but I said, 'No. I love you, but you're never going to see me again.'"

It took me a minute, but I got the point.

"But I'll tell you one thing," he continued. "As a cop, I've always trusted my instincts. I can't tell you more than that ..."

It was pouring rain still. If Matthew did come back, the likelihood of my giving him a place to stay for the night was about a hundred per cent.

But then there would be tomorrow night and the next night and the night after that ....

I thanked my friend. I got out of his car. I dashed through the rain to my door.

As soon as I got inside and took off my coat, the phone rang.

Matthew begged me to give him a bed for just one more night. "I have nowhere to go," he cried, not trying to hide the fact that he was now blatantly pleading with no pretense at all.

"Please," he said. "I've decided the best thing for me to do is to go up north and try to get my life back together. Just let me stay the night. Tomorrow I'll be gone. It makes perfect sense for me to spend just one more night with you."

"No. I'll meet you downtown and talk to you, but I will not let you come here," I swore. "I've been thinking about this all day and I ..."

"I bet you have. I just bet you've been thinking about this," he said with genuine nastiness. "Well, thanks, thanks a lot." He hung up.

I didn't feel sad or even relieved. I just felt empty. I felt that single, tiny conversation had proven beyond doubt that Matthew had cared nothing for me, had cared only about where he was going to lay his head each night, a head he kept clouded enough by drugs or alcohol or sex or madness to provide the dreams he surrendered to without resistance in the all-encompassing darkness of his sleep.

I went to sleep myself, not even very sad to be alone.

But I was awakened by the phone.

"Okay," he said, "just come downtown—wherever you like. Or we could meet at the Terminal …"

"No. Not in this neighbourhood."

"Okay. Just come downtown."

He needed enough money to spend the night in the baths, he said, and I promised to bring it to him.

His manner changed entirely. Gone was the nastiness. Now he was all sweetness again, swearing he loved me.

"Oh, Matthew, please," I said, sick of his nonsense. "You don't love me. You just need me …"

"No," he swore, "no. No. I …"

I interrupted any further protestations of devotion. "We can talk about that when I get there," I said with exasperation.

We met at the subway. I came up from the platform, and I saw him leaning against the tile wall of the Bloor Street station. He looked hateful—smirking and dirty and ugly. He looked like the stereotypical con artist: greasy, sneaky, bad.

I walked up to him, repelled, but full of a sense of power and adventure. In my purse was the difference between this man's sleeping in a doorway or a bed. In this desperate character off the filthy streets was a man more dangerous than any I'd known before, simply because he might be anyone: madman, conniver, thief, angel, devil, genius, singer, lover of women or men or both.

I should have been weeping and I would be soon, but now a wild laugh was chafing my lungs. I felt total contempt for Matthew and I felt strong.

"Where do you want to go to talk?" I asked, "Inside the subway or out?"

He smirked at me. "I know a place," he said, and he turned back toward the steps that led to the platform. We moved along it toward the concourse underneath Bloor and Yonge.

But before we even reached the steps—a distance of twenty or thirty feet, Matthew stopped. He seemed to suddenly change personality completely. As if something had come over him. Or as if something that had come over him before had suddenly been lifted.

CHAPTER TWENTY-TWO

He veered toward the yellow tile wall and threw his shoulder against it, pulling me toward him. His voice was broken and he began to tremble as his incoherent words forced themselves from his lips.

"Please," he cried, "please. If you have any shred of respect for me at all, you've got to believe that I really love you …"

As he spoke, his hands gyrated in the weird gestures he'd used the night he'd been delirious outside my window, having the effect of fending me off. "Please," he went on, "promise me you won't forget me—say you won't forget me."

I'd as likely forget myself, but I reassured him. He kept waving his hands in strange motions in front of his chest, and I finally told him to let me touch him. That stopped the frenetic movement. I tapped him lightly on the chest, not at all sure what my own gesture was meant to convey, though it must have intended some sort of comfort.

He calmed down a little. "I haven't got much time left," he said, "pretty soon I'm going to be dead."

All I could think of was what the cop had said about Matthew being a guy on the way down. "Yes," I answered, "I know."

"So you've got to believe I love you. Because I'm going to die."

I tried to calm him. But he switched out of this personality into a sort of neutral one, leading us down through the subway concourse toward a dark, dingy bar at the farthest extremity of the underground plaza.

Of course, as he had no money, he asked if I would buy beer and cigarettes, which I did.

We sat on tall stools at the end of the bar. By now it was midnight, and there were only a few people in the bar. Everyone could hear the wild talk that issued from Matthew and the wild tears and protestations that issued from me.

He said he was going up north to wander into the wild to kill himself. He said that meeting me and loving me was a cruel irony because he hadn't loved anyone for two years. At that time, he said, he had had a wonderful career, but—realizing he could never have children—he had finally become totally unable to continue because it just wasn't worth it to him. He said he had simply walked out on his life.

He claimed to have had plenty of money and said he had simply taken to roaming—that he had been to Europe. He mentioned Budapest, which I had told him I particularly loved. He said, "I have been to Buda and I have been to Pest," which he pronounced "Pesht." Most people have no idea that Budapest is really these two cities and that the name of the second is pronounced as though it contained an h. How did he know these things? How did he know that I knew them and that I would be impressed? I never spoke of the separate cities or used the proper pronunciation myself.

He told me that he had once been a much better man than he was now. He said that once he'd been cultured and respectable.

It was certainly true that he looked shabby now. His wonderful hair, though still clean, had somehow become too long and had lost its style. His coat was minus its belt, so it hung on his slender frame like something that has escaped the wind and swings on a twig. His shoes were ruined by so very many days and nights of rain. His complexion seemed blotchy. He even needed to blow his nose.

But his conversation, though desperate and strange, was as compelling as ever. He said, "Sometimes fantasy and reality are confused in my head." He swore over and over that he was a broken man, that once he had been something, that now he was nothing, that without the ability to have children, his life was worthless.

"But you could adopt ..." I protested.

"How could I adopt a child?" he asked. He said his father had told him that by walking away from his career in bitterness over his inability to have children, he was ruining his opportunity to adopt. He laughed at the irony of that.

Over and over he repeated there was nothing for him to do but to go up north and kill himself.

Desperately, I tried to convince him that he was wrong. That he was a wonderful person, that he had every chance in the world to go on with life, to improve.

But he said he couldn't. He said, "There was no morality to things before; now there is ..."

I didn't know what he was talking about. What he meant by morality. What he meant by "now."

He kept on and on and soon I was throwing my arms around his neck and begging him not to kill himself.

It made a delicious spectacle for the bartender and the other customers—all of whom were watching with rapt interest.

"You don't know what shameless really means," he said "You don't know what I have done in the last two years …"

"Lying?" I said, "stealing?"

"Well," he answered softly, "lying and—no—well, yes—stealing."

He looked into my eyes. "There's one thing, though," he said, "one thing you've got to believe. I've been with countless women in my time, and you are truly beautiful. You have to believe that you are a truly beautiful woman."

Despite the tears, I smiled. He was not going to make me believe that. All the other men who'd sworn I was truly beautiful had not made me believe it either.

We must have talked for forty minutes or so. Matthew tried hard to convince me that he must die, that there was no way he could change or improve his life. Once, he said, he'd worked for an Italian couple as a dishwasher but he'd eventually had to walk away from that, too. He was finished. There was nothing more to be done but to die.

Wearily, I agreed. Death did seem the only solution. For the first time in my life, the suicide of someone seemed to make perfect sense.

I came to this conclusion at about the same time as the bartender came over to tell us he was closing up. As he took away our glasses and ashtray and wiped the bar, he smirked at Matthew and laughed merrily and said, "Goodbye then—until next time."

Matthew told me that this was a place where he drank when he was "in Toronto." I suddenly understood it was also a place where he must say goodbye to girlfriends who'd outlived their usefulness.

We left the bar and walked out into the concourse, now nearly deserted in the slimy subterranean downtown wee hours. We found a pay phone nearby and called information and got the number of the friend he said he was going to up north in Killaloe.

I offered to stay downtown with him—in a hotel. I wanted to spend as much of his remaining time together as we could. I really believed his story about walking away from a brilliant career. I really thought he'd reached the end of his rope. I really believed he was going to die.

CHAPTER TWENTY-THREE

FINALLY, IDIOTICALLY, I BEGAN to insist that he come back home with me. Once more, I threw my arms around his neck and wept. He embraced me, holding me to him and making no attempt to push me away despite my clinging to him. A group of men—possibly from the bar—walked by and sarcastically called out, "Cute couple!"

But I didn't care. All I cared about now was my few remaining hours with Matthew.

All he cared about, after smiling and protesting weakly, "Against my better judgment," was the fact that I was paying for a cab—the subway now closed—and taking him home for one more night.

The minute we got inside the cab, all talk of love and death ceased. Matthew got home, got undressed and fell asleep nearly at once, but not before telling me one more time that he had really got the work writing the jingles.

Suddenly I became convinced that the whole weird speech about his having walked away from a brilliant career was yet another lie. That his remorse over his wasted life was a lie. I began to get all screwed up. Was he lying when he said he was a terrible asshole? Yes? But then he wasn't an asshole? But he was a liar?

I lay awake all night trying to figure out unfigurable conundrums and trying to decide whether I should fear for my life. Not because Matthew was dangerously insane but because I was dangerously stupid.

In the morning I told him how terrified I'd been the whole time I'd been with him. He listened and he apologized. I told him I'd gone to the police. I told him about my conversation with the cop the night before and what that cop had told me about people ripping people off, and people on the way down and loving and walking away. Matthew's answer to this was, "It sounds like you've got a good friend in that guy …"

I told him the police had told me—which was true—that he was way off in his estimates of how long funds took to get from the States to Toronto. I smiled and warned him to be more careful the next time he used that technique to get money from a woman. He seemed to be holding his breath, to be listening very hard to what I was saying.

I mentioned a few other things about his technique as a shyster and I said, "You'd make a far better one—a perfect one—Matthew, if you could just get over being so very nervous right before you ask for the money." He said nothing.

I knew, too, that there was but a single bus to Killaloe each day, and that I was determined that Matthew should be on it. We continued to talk as though he were about to commit suicide, and I, who, in the emotional turmoil of the evening before had considered alerting someone to stop him—even, perhaps, trying to locate his parents—was now feeling that if that was what he'd decided to do, then that was what he should do.

Half of me believed he really wanted to die. The other half just wanted him out of my life. He might be tired of being a gigolo, a shyster, a liar. I was tired of being afraid.

I convinced him that time was running out, that he should phone his friends in Killaloe to make sure they still lived there. I wanted to make sure he really had someone to go to.

He rose and dialed the number. As always, his voice on the phone was deep, confident, commanding—the voice of a successful, self-assured man.

He spoke for only a few moments, telling his friends he'd be coming their way and was planning on dropping by. I signaled for him to give me the phone, which he did without resistance.

When I took the receiver, I spoke to the man by the last name Matthew had told me was the man's to make sure that that was indeed the person Matthew had called. I no longer trusted him at all. I wouldn't have been the least surprised if the voice on the other end had belonged to a recording, or if, in fact, there might be no voice at all.

But the man answered to the name. And since I had watched every digit Matthew had dialed, I knew the man had to actually be up north.

I wanted to warn him that Matthew was suicidal, but, since Matthew was sitting beside me, this was difficult. I settled for a cryptic sentence to the effect that the man should keep an eye on Matthew if he should wander into the woods. I said something about spring fever.

I don't know why, but I was surprised that the man sounded at least a little annoyed at the prospect of Matthew's planning on visiting him. He said whatever Matthew did was his own business as he, himself, was far too busy with work on his own place to bother about Matthew.

I hung up a little confused, but relieved that at least Matthew was headed for someone who really existed.

It seemed a foregone conclusion that it was I who would be buying the ticket.

When Matthew got ready to go, I asked him if he would take something of mine with him, and he said that he hoped I would let him take an unusual and very beautiful sweatshirt that my brother had given me in Utica and which I'd let Matthew wear a couple of times. It was black with a striking design on the front in white, against which was silhouetted the black head of a loon with a red eye. Beneath were the words, "Loon Magic." I knew there were very few such sweatshirts in existence, since they were available only from a very small and obscure printer in New York State. I knew this might be the only one in all of Canada.

Matthew looked magnificent in this exotic piece of clothing, which complemented perfectly the dark, long, clean curls, the pale fine-boned lines of his face. I was happy to let him have it, even though I'd never had a chance to wear it myself except to try it on.

In return, he left the panther sweater—which he swore he had bought in New York City for six hundred and fifty dollars.

Just before we left, he began the little whining sound I recognized as the voice of a begger. "No, Matthew," I had to tell him, "I can't give you any more money."

We left for the bus terminal. I had called in sick at work again and therefore wasn't in a hurry to get to the office. But though the bus didn't leave until one, it was barely eleven. Far too early—but I wanted to make very sure that we weren't too late for Matthew to get on that bus.

All the way downtown, he sat very close to me, our thighs touching, just as we had every other day.

By the time we got to the terminal, we still had an hour to wait for the bus. Matthew was terribly nervous. I was scared, tired and confused. It was a warm, beautiful sunny day—as if once more the season had changed. Despite our mutual state, we noticed, even enjoyed this strange, sudden, untimely summer.

CHAPTER TWENTY-FOUR

At the bus terminal, I kept waiting for Matthew to disappear. I just expected to turn around and find him gone. At one point, I did turn around and did find him missing—but only because he had moved closer to me.

It took only moments to buy the ticket, since it was midday Tuesday and the terminal was nearly empty. We decided to go for a beer, and Matthew chose a place across the street from the terminal. He seemed to know every bar in town. We sat facing a window that looked out on Bay Street. We discussed the old, questionable-looking hotel across the street. I asked—half-joking—whether Matthew had ever been in there. I was now so terrified about what he had told me the night before about roaming and sleeping in the gay baths—which he said he'd done in Paris, Montréal, and New York as well as Toronto, supplying details of how the men cruised at night and how each city had its own code by which straight men who slept in the baths let it be known they weren't available.

Of course, he had told me that he'd never been available in that way, but I now considered him capable of anything I was capable of imagining.

A tall man walked by us—inside the bar—and it seemed to me that Matthew glanced at him with a hint of desire. Once again I asked him whether he had ever slept with a man. He shook his head seriously and said, "Never in my life."

Then he smiled and added, "But I've thought about it ..."

He went on. "When I was reading about ancient Greece," he said, "I read that there a man could do whatever he felt like doing sexually until he was thirty. Then, he had to choose whether he would be gay or straight for the rest of his life. That is so much more civilized than us. I wish we were as civilized as that."

It struck me that the word "civilized" had been one of Matthew's favourites during our brief time together. It also struck me that I was becoming more terrified by the moment at Matthew's apparent sexual ambiguity.

"Oh, Matthew," I sighed, "I really hope you haven't lied to me about everything—about being sterile ..."

Again he smiled, completely without rancour and said, "Well, in a month you'll know about that, won't you?"

He sipped his beer and glanced out the window. He was not sad, but he was very pale and shaky. He looked small and distant and clean again and handsome. I knew I had less than an hour left to be with him. I wanted the hour to go. I wanted him to go.

He ordered two more beers at once and drank them fast. I ordered one and drank it quickly, too. Outside, an old man passed by, a Chinese man walking with one arm behind his back. Matthew commented on how civilized the old man looked. Again that word. He seemed to be going away. Seemed to have left me already.

We went outside and walked in the sun. As on the very first afternoon, Matthew looked over at my hair and laughed sweetly.

"What is it?" I was laughing, too. Despite the terrible weirdness of what was going on, we kept slipping back into the laughing warmth we'd shared for so many happy hours. He said, as he had said the first time I'd walked with him, "The colour of your hair looks neat in the sun."

I thought about circles—how we walk in them all the days of our lives, how we turn back upon ourselves, how we spin and spin.

We went back to the bus terminal to check the time but it was still too early. The racing minutes dragged their feet. We walked back out into the sun again and headed to yet another bar across the street.

I had a Perrier and Matthew downed another two beers and he talked about our relationship, saying he had enjoyed our time out of bed as much as our time in bed—saying again, too, that he wished he'd met me before things had gone bad with him.

But there was a flatness to everything he said, and I was unable to know whether it was because he was really thinking he would kill himself soon and was upset, or whether the strangeness of what was happening was affecting him. Nor could I be sure my own ears were capable of hearing clearly, so strong was the fear and the sorrow, the longing and regret. I wanted him to stay forever and to get away as soon as possible.

He told me again that he had once given a solo concert to which his parents had come. He told me that it was true he once had had a very fine career. The bar we sat in now was quite elegant. A lunchtime crowd calmly ate their meal, totally unaware of the couple at the chrome and glass bar. Us. Almost done. Done for.

I kept looking at my watch. Finally I told Matthew we had to go and he tossed down the rest of his fourth beer. We headed for the terminal. As we crossed the street, he said, "On my way to the oblivion express ..." But a laugh was bubbling up through the hysteria in both of us.

When we got to the terminal, he asked me if I would buy him some cigarettes and I was happy to do him this one last favour. I asked him what I should ask for and he told me and I got him a couple of packs.

Out on the platform, he asked me if I would give him some money for "one last blow-out in Killaloe," and I told him no. He reached into the pocket of his coat and pulled out the contents—a few tattered business cards, including my own, and a five-dollar bill. I didn't give him anything more to add to this ragged beggar collection.

It seemed to take forever for the bus to load, but at long last, the line began to move. Matthew turned to me, grabbed hold of me, held me to him and said, "I really do love you."

Tiredly, not knowing whether I meant it or not, I answered, "I love you, too."

Finally, it came to be his turn to board. He turned and said goodbye and disappeared into the blackness of the bus.

I was so afraid he would hop back off if I left the platform that I was determined to stay until the bus pulled out.

It seemed to be hours. I waited and waited, standing there in the deserted bay with only Matthew's bus yet to leave and only me seeing it off. The driver fussed with luggage, chatted with other drivers, came, went, came back, got on, got off—

And all the time, I waited for Matthew to roll out of my life. I could see nothing, because the windows of the bus were so darkly tinted. I thought he might be sitting on the other side of the bus, so I walked around it once, but felt silly and started to laugh.

Then I worried that he might have fled the bus while I was on the side away from the door—even though the door had only been out of my sight for moments.

Then, it was time. The bus driver was ready, and he began to pull out. As he did so, I saw a figure on the bus rise and become visible standing in the aisle. The figure waved and I saw by the motion of its hand and by its posture that it was Matthew waving goodbye.

I waved, too, and watched as the bus drew away from the terminal bay.

CHAPTER TWENTY-FIVE

AND ONLY WHEN I could see the bus no longer did I turn and walk off the platform, back through the waiting room, out onto the sidewalk, across the street, past the bar we'd just been in, down the sidewalk we'd just walked, toward the subway we'd just ridden, and all the way back to the basement room we'd shared for the past seventeen days.

I had come all the way back in a trance, and the moment I entered, Matthew's permanent absence hit me like a fist in the chest. I drew in a stunned breath. Whatever had happened in this room was over forever and would never happen again.

Still in a trance, but one now more comprised of sorrow than relief, I saw the panther sweater draped carefully over the chair where Matthew had sat so many times, where I'd taken his dark curls between my confident hands.

I took the sweater straight to the sink and began to wash it. I'd not noticed that it was a little threadbare. I washed it and washed it as Lady Macbeth had washed her bloody key. But I wasn't washing Matthew out of it. I was washing away anything that might in any way damage or diminish it because I had decided to keep it forever.

Carefully, I laid it out to dry.

And then I lay down myself.

And over me began to wash wave after wave of revulsion. I thought of all of Matthew's lies. I thought of the drugs, the fevered sex, the talk about gay men, the baths, the streets, the craziness that poured out of him when he was begging me to hold him, never to leave him. I thought of his terrifying fragility, of his complete poverty, of his wasted talent and his conniving life.

And I thought how he had tricked and duped and fooled me. How he had told me I was beautiful. How he had sworn over and over that he loved me, then taken a whole month's salary away from me. I thought of the way he smelled the night he'd met me at midnight at the bus terminal that terrible Sunday. I thought of him digging in the ashtray for a butt, the way any bum would. I thought of his waking in the middle of the night to smoke a cigarette, then collapsing into a stupor again.

I thought of him as a weak, cheating, crazy, ugly vagrant living off the desperation of decent women past their prime.

I thought of ways he might even now be trying to rob me. Credit cards. Bank cards. Cheques. Long distance calls.

I thought of disease. Of many of them. Of the worst.

I lay for hours as the soft sun through my basement windows gave into darkness. I thought I had been so stupid as to not merit the pity of decent people and so soiled as to never expect to be granted social intercourse—let alone any other kind—ever again.

For days, all I could think of was how horrible everything about Matthew had been. In the middle of the first night he was gone, I heard the phone ring. I awoke and lay stock-still, hearing his voice on the machine saying he would call me back.

The next morning, he did call, and I answered. He said he was at the Toronto bus terminal. It was nine a.m. The once-a-day bus from Killaloe wouldn't arrive until 3 p.m. Clearly, he had not gone there.

He said he'd decided that knowing me had given him the strength not to want to commit suicide after all.

I said nothing. I was not moved. I was afraid this call meant he would come back to my place. I was scared.

He asked me whether he had hurt me and I said, "I don't think you have to worry about that."

Angrily he replied, "Yes, I do."

I said to him, "You know we can never see each other again."

He said, "Yes."

I asked him never to come to my place again, and—a little insulted—he said, "Of course not."

He said that all he wanted to do now was to pick up the pieces of his life.

I simply said, "Matthew, I wish you all the luck in the world." And then I hung up and I went to work.

As the days went by, I grew more and more frantically afraid that Matthew had tried to rob me somehow. I began frenetic calls to my credit card company, to my bank, to the phone company to check these things out.

And I also began to check every day to see whether the panther sweater, which I had hung on the door of my washroom, had somehow disappeared of its own accord.

I felt dirty and wanton and foolish and old.

But something besides this horrible self-loathing began to happen. I began to miss Matthew. I began to miss him as passionately as I had once missed him—in the days in which I could count the hours until I would be seeing him again. I could count the hours now, too. They numbered all the hours of my life, for much as I feared he would return, much as I shook with fear at the thought of some night coming home and finding him crouched at my window, I knew he would never come back to me.

The long, long days went on. It seemed that many had passed before he called me again, but actually, it was in the middle of the night between the first Friday and the first Saturday that he was gone—only a few days after he left—that the machine intercepted a call from him again. He said, "Hello, Marie, I just wanted to say hello."

My heart sang at the sound of his voice. I was still terrified, but I longed for him so, that I played the tape over and over again, just to hear those eight words.

The next day was a rainy, dismal Sunday. I folded the panther sweater—which had not disappeared—and put it away. I spent the long day alone, as I had spent so many Sundays before he came.

At six—the hour at which he'd so often called me before—the phone rang.

"Hello," he said, "this is Matthew."

"I know."

His voice was very broken and really sounded as though he were in tears. "I just wanted you to know," he said, "that I am extremely sorry for what happened. Somewhere along the line, I got off the track ..."

There was a long silence. My heart closed, as though this were not happening at all, as though I had no feeling left in me. Finally, though, I forced myself to say, "Well, thank you for telling me that; I really appreciate it."

There was another pause. "I just wanted to say goodbye," he said, his voice still sounding as though he spoke with great difficulty.

Somehow, I could not keep a smile out of my own voice. It was a smile of relief that he was gone. It was a smile of gratitude that he had been noble enough to call. It was a smile of well-wishing. It was a smile of a kind of love. "Goodbye, Matthew," I said, too blithely, too easily. And I hung up the phone. I felt almost nothing, except that I thought it was very nice of him to have called.

CHAPTER TWENTY-SIX

THE FIRST THING I learned was that I was not pregnant.

Then I learned that Matthew had not tried to rob, pilfer, or cheat me out of anything except the money he had asked for and had been freely given.

Each time that I checked and found that Matthew had not hurt me in some way I had suspected, my hurt over the loss of him became more acute.

There remained only to find out whether he had in some way infected me.

When the day came, I found myself sitting in the blood testing laboratory when an old female patient walked in and sat in a neighbouring chair, all cheerful and friendly and nice. I almost expected her to ask me—in a small-talk sort of way—what I was being tested for and I was almost prepared to say, "Oh, well, I fell in love with this vagrant who is possibly bi-sexual so I thought it made good sense to be tested for AIDS …."

She never asked.

So I just sat there and watched as the virginal technician approached me and punched a hole in my arm and waited for five glass vials to fill quickly with my blood. And as I watched those fat glass tubes turn red, I thought what a tough old muscle is my good heart.

Several weeks later, the doctor phoned to say that all the tests were negative.

I wept. Matthew now seemed officially—well and truly—gone from my life. And all the harm he had done, as far as anyone could tell, was to let me love him, then to go when I sent him away. I longed for him as never before. Though I knew that what I longed for would never be mine—or anyone's—because Matthew was a myth.

There had been times when I had feared that I would find him again someday. Sleeping on a subway grate. Hunched in a doorway. Wandering some ward I was doing volunteer work in or dragged into some courtroom where I was observing a trial.

But as I realized for one last time that he had not robbed, raped, defiled, seduced, impregnated or infected me, I felt the certain knowledge that I would never see Matthew again. I wondered what it would be like to love like a widow.

It was now the latter part of June, again a Sunday, and the bright spring warmth of March had given way to the heat of summer.

I was down at the harbour, sitting on a bench, idly watching the yachts and smaller craft negotiating the turns necessary to get out onto the wide free waters of the lake. There were people walking on the path behind me. I could hear their conversations, the idle chatter of families and friends enjoying the leisure of a day off.

I was happy for them, happy for them all. As for myself, I was content to watch the boats and to read my book and to enjoy my own leisure.

I don't know how long I had sat there when I heard it. At first I thought it must be my imagination. Behind me came the voices of a couple. She sounded sophisticated, an educated woman, but friendly, too. She spoke of her love of the lake and how much she enjoyed sharing time beside it with a new friend.

The man said, "Well, as I'll only be in town for a couple of weeks working in the studio, I appreciate any time I can spend relaxing. "And," he added, "finding a woman like you to spend it with, that makes it really special."

Whatever the woman said in reply, I couldn't hear. But I heard him again, and this time I knew who it was who spoke.

"It's nearly one now," he said, "and I really should be getting back. But I'll be done at about eight-thirty."

"Oh," the woman replied, hesitantly, hopefully, I thought.

"So maybe we can meet. Have a little supper …"

"I guess that would be okay. Yes. That would be fine."

There was a silence as if she were wondering exactly what or where he had in mind.

"Listen," he finally said. "I know a cute little place in the west end. I'd like to meet you there, treat you to a beer or two …"

The woman laughed. "I'm not really a beer drinker, but …"

"You'll love the place. It's called The Lakeview Restaurant. You can wait for me …"

"I don't usually sit alone in a bar," the woman answered. "I find that sort of scary."

"No," I heard the man reply in his soft, persuasive voice. "Not scary at all. A beautiful woman like you has no need to be afraid. Someone will always look after you."

I didn't turn. I didn't watch them as they walked away.

For a good long time, I watched the boats speed out of the harbour and toward the adventure of the deep open waters. Then I closed my book, stood up, walked away and, with a smile of relief and forgiveness, lost myself in the crowd.

Acknowledgements

I would like to acknowledge the support of the Quattro crew, especially John Calabro and Allan Briesmaster. And I say a special thanks to my husband, Douglas Purdon.

Other Quattro Fiction

Texas by Claudio Gaudio
Abundance of the Infinite by Christopher Canniff
The Proxy Bride by Terri Favro
Tea with the Tiger by Nathan Unsworth
A Certain Grace by Binnie Brennan
Life Without by Ken Klonsky
Romancing the Buzzard by Leah Murray
The Lebanese Dishwasher by Sonia Saikaley
Against God by Patrick Senécal
The Ballad of Martin B. by Michael Mirolla
Mahler's Lament by Deborah Kirshner
Surrender by Peter Learn
Constance, Across by Richard Cumyn
In the Mind's Eye by Barbara Ponomareff
The Panic Button by Koom Kankesan
Shrinking Violets by Heidi Greco
Grace by Vanessa Smith
Break Me by Tom Reynolds
Retina Green by Reinhard Filter
Gaze by Keith Cadieux
Tobacco Wars by Paul Seesequasis
The Sea by Amela Marin
Real Gone by Jim Christy
A Gardener on the Moon by Carole Giangrande
Good Evening, Central Laundromat by Jason Heroux
Of All the Ways To Die by Brenda Niskala
The Cousin by John Calabro
Harbour View by Binnie Brennan
The Extraordinary Event of Pia H. by Nicola Vulpe
A Pleasant Vertigo by Egidio Coccimiglio
Wit in Love by Sky Gilbert
The Adventures of Micah Mushmelon by Michael Wex
Room Tone by Gale Zoë Garnett